In the Distance, and Ahead in Time

In the Distance, and Ahead in Time

George Zebrowski

Five Star • Waterville, Maine

Five Star First Edition Science Fiction and Fantasy Series.

Published in 2002 in conjunction with Tekno-Books and Ed Gorman.

Set in 11 pt. Plantin by Ramona A. Watson.

Printed in the United States on permanent paper.

Library of Congress Cataloging-in-Publication Data

Zebrowski, George, 1945–
In the distance, and ahead in time : stories / by George Zebrowski.
p. cm.—(Five Star first edition science fiction and fantasy series)
Contents: The water sculptor — Parks of rest and culture — Assassins of air — The soft and terrible music — The sea of evening — Heathen god — Wayside world — In the distance, and ahead in time — Transfigured night — Between the winds.
ISBN 0-7862-4687-1 (hc : alk. paper)
1. Science fiction, American. I. Title. II. Series.
PS3576.E35 I5 2002
8113′.54—dc21 2002029726

To W. Warren Wagar,
Hero of my youth,
Friend of my middle age,
Who helped me think.

Table of Contents

Introduction

Stories and novels are an author's mindchildren. They grow slowly, and you write every line of their DNA yourself! Whatever is wrong stays wrong, but what inspired you to write them also remains. As with biological progeny, there are elements that are beyond your control, and it is that unpredictable creativity that will make them interesting to read.

A short story is a lonely voice, not easily heard these days, and certainly not the most important thing that goes on in the world. It brings to the reader a brief design and voices that strive to be heard within that brief design, much like the instruments in a string quartet. Read too quickly and you may miss the subtleties.

In addition to the voices of its characters, a science fiction story should also voice thoughts, and so requires a thoughtful reader; or at least one open to the seductions of thinking, to the beauties of an idea or a rounded bit of reasoning, as much as to the trills of emotion and the thrills of action. A science fiction story without thought must surely be a lesser science fiction story—or perhaps not a science fiction story at all.

These stories had this kind of reader, now and then, in the editors who published them and in the reviewers and readers who saw enough in the stories to comment on them. They were usually lone reactions (I rarely had more than one for each story), but they seemed to hear the inner voices within each story's design and language.

Design, language, and the thoughts and emotions expressed by people. These are the ingredients of true science fiction stories, with thoughts being the distinctive characteristic, like musical structures balanced against the actions.

"The Water Sculptor" was my first published story. I took it with me to the first Clarion Writers Workshop in 1968. An editor at Charles Scribner's Sons in New York later saw it in a proposed but never published collection of stories from that workshop, and invited me to lunch. He gave me my first contract for my novel, *Macrolife* (1979), which was published by Harper & Row after that editor left Scribner's. Still, this was the story that called me to the attention of a major publisher, when it was still unpublished and a bit devalued in my mind by two rejections by major markets. I had also foolishly let my brother and his girlfriend read the story. "Who do you think you are?" she said. "Too serious to be published," he said.

I remember dropping it off to the editor of a paperback anthology series on my way to my summer job with the New York City Parks Department. My brother was with me that day, on his way to the same summer job, and I knew from the looks he gave me that he was wondering what I could possibly expect from such behavior. I got a quick letter back from the editor asking for some revisions. I saw the virtues in the requests, did the revisions in about two hours the next day, and again delivered the story personally, alone, on my way to work. Another letter informed me that the editor liked the story, and I would hear by October whether the story was going to be included in the anthology. A check arrived well before October; and then one day, a few weeks before Christmas, as I was bringing home some laundry to my off-campus college apartment, I saw a package stuck in my mailbox.

I dropped my laundry on the porch, reached for the package, opened it clumsily—and there it was! *Infinity One*, a paperback anthology. I turned to the contents page and there was my name by the story. I simply stood there, trying to absorb the fact that I had done it.

I immediately took the story over to the hospital, where Pamela Sargent, my lifelong companion, was in for some repairs.

"What's this?" she asked, looking pale and tired but beautiful with her long dark hair strewn prettily over the pillow.

"Take a look," I said.

She looked and said, "Oh, a collection. Thanks."

"Look closer," I said, "—at the contents page."

She looked, and the puzzled expression on her face changed to a smile—and that moment on the porch with all my laundry repeated itself in a much better way.

"I'll leave the collection with you," I said.

"Aw—okay," she said, and I wondered whether she was looking at me differently.

Nearly a hundred stories later, there has been nothing like that doubled moment, although there have been moments. A writer has only a limited number of "firsts" in his working life, so don't let them pass by too quickly. Remember how little it took to be happy with one story. In all fairness to my brother's girlfriend, she spoke to me decades later, and said, "Who knew!"

The story received praise and a Nebula recommendation from James Tiptree, Jr., and from Jerry Pournelle—two very different writers. The story certainly owes to the work of Arthur C. Clarke. It also presents the problem of orbital space junk, which continues to get worse.

I returned to Christian Praeger's adventures in "Parks of Rest and Culture" and in "Assassins of Air," to find out how he crossed paths with the "water sculptor."

"Heathen God" was my fourth published story. Barry Malzberg's "author's workout" series of springboards and sketches for writers in the *SFWA Bulletin* provided the impetus. I added quite a bit to this sketch, but Barry's spirit was somehow holding my hand all the way. The story was partly written in my head during my summer job for the New York City Parks Department, and "remembered" onto paper scene by scene whenever I had the chance. It was a Nebula Award finalist and was included in *Nebula Awards Seven* (Harper & Row, 1972), and is my most reprinted and translated story. I went to the awards banquet in New York City, happy to be a nominee, knowing that I was not getting first place. Friends of mine attended: also my mother, to see what I was doing with my life; my brother, who ducked out early, just after I introduced him to Lester del Rey, an author he had read. I introduced my mother to Isaac Asimov, who hugged her; to James Gunn, who thanked her for producing me; and to Harlan Ellison, who was nonplussed—probably because my mother always looked and acted like a cross between Marilyn Monroe (the blonde look) and Zsa Zsa Gabor (the European accent).

"The Soft Terrible Music" I wrote for John DeChancie's and Martin Greenberg's collection *Castle Fantastic* because I was in love with two things at the time: the "warm" valley in Antarctica, where I thought it would be nice to have a house; and the idea of a spatially extended house—an idea that goes back to Robert A. Heinlein's wonderful 1940 story, "And He Built a Crooked House." Themes of love and revenge crept into my story. Expensive houses in protected and exotic places often have great crimes associated with them. John DeChancie wrote me an enthusiastic reaction to the story, in which he described the story as being of "the true quill."

"The Sea of Evening" proposes an answer to Fermi's Paradox, which asks: if the universe is full of intelligent life, then where are they? Why haven't we been contacted? My story, which also owes a bit to Arthur C. Clarke's "The Nine Billion Names of God" in its technique, gives one answer to Enrico Fermi. Konstantin Tsiolkovsky asked the same question many years before Fermi, and also gave an intriguing answer. I tend to think there may be several answers to the question, rather than one.

Poul Anderson created a world named Cleopatra out of basic astronomical and physical possibilities, as an imaginary planet circling a distant star. He then wrote a long story set there, and a number of new writers added stories and lore for the collection, each playing with Anderson's carefully wrought backdrop. I took the opportunity to have this world's existence intersect with my own Macrolife mosaic of stories and novels about mobile, self-reproducing habitats. Poul, who had also done some background work for me in part one of *Macrolife*, was delighted, and even suggested that I might make a larger work from "Wayside World."

"In the Distance, and Ahead in Time" is more directly in the Macrolife mosaic; the people of the mobile habitat arrive at the beginning of the story rather than at its end, and cause all sorts of ethical/political problems, not to mention personal difficulties for my characters. Yet the issues of land expropriation are very much still with us, beginning with just about every human migration of history, to the violent seizure and settling of North America, to the Middle East. I wrote this story for my friend Chad Oliver, whose anthropological science fiction remains without peer.

Contrary to fashionable amnesia, the idea of virtual reality is far from new. It fades into modern science fiction from the 19th and 20th centuries, through such books as *Peter Ibbetson* (1891) by George Du Maurier, Laurence Manning's 1933 story, "The City of Sleep," James Gunn's *The Joy Makers* (1961), Daniel Galouye's brilliant *Counterfeit World* (1964), and many others. The wish takes on practical reality through today's computer engineering human interface ideas. "Transfigured Night" was how I was getting there with this theme. "Between the Winds" takes the theme to one ultimate result, as humanity voyages into sea changes.

Ten stories.

Ten dreamtimes out of my life, when I was happy to write them down.

—George Zebrowski
Spring 2002

Near Futures

The Water Sculptor

Sitting there, watching the Earth below him from the panel of Station Six, Christian Praeger suddenly felt embarrassed by the planet's beauty. For the last eight hours he had watched the great storm develop in the Pacific, and he had wanted to share the view with someone, tell someone how beautiful he thought it was. He had told it to himself now for the fiftieth time.

The storm was a physical evil, a spinning hell that might reach the Asian mainland and kill thousands of starving billions. They would get a warning, for all the good that would do. Since the turn of the century there had been dozens of such storms, developing in places way off from the traditional storm cradles.

He looked at the delicate pinwheel. It was a part of the planet's ecology—whatever state that was in now. The arms of the storm reminded him of the theory which held the galaxy to be a kind of organized storm system which sucked in gas and dust at its center and sent it all out into the vast arms to condense into stars. And the stars were stormy laboratories building the stuff of the universe in the direction of huge molecules, from the inanimate and crystalline to the living and conscious. In the slowness of time it all looked stable, Praeger thought, but almost certainly all storms run down and die.

He looked at the clock above the center screen. There were six clocks around the watch room, one above each screen. The clock on the ceiling gave station time. His watch would be over in half an hour.

He looked at the sun screen. There all the dangerous rays were filtered out. He turned up the electronic magnification and for a long time watched the prominences flare up and die. He looked at the cancerous sunspots. The sight was hypnotic and frightening no matter how many times he had seen it. He put his hand out to the computer panel and punched in the routine information. Then he looked at the spectroscopic screens, small rectangles beneath the Earth watch monitors. He checked the time, and set the automatic release for the ozone scatter-cannisters to be dropped into the atmosphere. A few minutes later he watched them drop away from the station, following their fall until they broke in the upper atmosphere, releasing the precious ozone that would protect Earth's masses from the sun's deadly radiation. Early in the twentieth century a good deal of the natural ozone layer in the upper atmosphere had been stripped away as a result of atomic testing and the use of aerosol sprays, resulting in much genetic damage in the late eighties and nineties. But soon now the ozone layer would be back up to snuff.

When his watch ended ten minutes later, Praeger was glad to get away from the visual barrage of the screens. He made his way into one of the jutting spokes of the station where his sleep cubicle was located. Here it was a comfortable half-g all the time. He settled himself into his bunk, and pushed the music button at his side, leaving his small observation and com screen on the ceiling turned off. Gradually the music filled the room and he closed his eyes. Mahler's weary song of Earth's misery enveloped his consciousness with pity and weariness, and love. Before he fell asleep he wished he might feel the Earth's atmosphere the way he felt his own skin.

I wish I could hear and feel the motion of gas molecules in the upper air, the whisperings of subtle energy transfers . . .

In the Pacific, weather control engineers guided the great storm into an electrostatic basket. The storm would provide usable power for the rest of its natural life.

Praeger awoke a quarter of an hour before his watch was due to begin. He thought of his recent vacation Earthside, remembering the glowing volcano he had seen in Italy, and how strange the silver shield of the Moon had looked through Earth's atmosphere. He remembered watching his own station six, his post in life, moving slowly across the sky; remembered one of the inner stations as it passed Julian's station 233, one of the few private satellites, synchronous, fixed for all time over one point on the Earth. He should be able to talk to Julian soon, during his next off period. Even though Julian was an artist and a recluse, a water sculptor as he called himself, Julian and he were very much alike. At times he felt they were each other's conscience, two ex-spacemen in continual retreat from their home world. It was much more beautiful, and bearable from out here. In all this silence he sometimes thought he could hear the universe breathing. It was alive, the whole starry cosmos throbbing.

If I could tear a hole in its body, it would bleed and cry out for a bandage . . .

He remembered the stifling milieu of Rome's streets: the great screens which went dead during his vacation, blinding the city, the crowds waiting on the stainless steel squares for the music to resume over the giant audios. They could not work without it. The music pounded its monotonous bass beat: the sound of some imprisoned beast beneath the city. The cab that waited for him was a welcome sight: an instrument for fleeing.

In the shuttle craft that brought him back to station six he read the little quotation printed on the back of every seat for the ten thousandth time; it told him that the shuttle dated back to the building of the giant Earth station system.

". . . What we are building now is the nervous system of mankind . . . the communications network of which the satellites will be the nodal points. They will enable the consciousness of our grandchildren to flicker like lightning back and forth across the face of the planet . . ."

Praeger got up from his bunk and made his way back to the watch room. He was glad now to get away from his own thoughts and return to the visual stimulation of the watch screens. Soon he would be talking to Julian again; they would share each other's friendship in the universe of the spoken word as they shared a silent past every time they looked at each other across the void.

Julian's large green eyes reminded him each time of the view out by Neptune, the awesome size of the sea green giant, the ship outlined against it, and the fuel tank near it blossoming into a red rose, silently; the first ship had been torn in half. Julian had been in space, coming over to Praeger's command ship when it happened, to pick up a spare part for the radio-telescope. *They* blamed Julian because *they* had to blame someone. After all, he had been in command. Chances were that something had already gone wrong, and that nothing could have stopped it. Only one man had been lost.

Julian and Praeger were barred from taking any more missions, unfairly, they thought. There were none coming up that either of them would have been interested in anyway, but at the time they put up a fight. Some fool official said publicly that they were unfit to represent mankind beyond the solar system—a silly thing to say, especially when the UN had just put a ban on extra-solar activities. They were threatened with dishonorable discharges, but they were also world heroes; the publicity would have been embarrassing.

Julian believed that most of mankind was unfit for just about everything. With his small fortune and the backing of patrons he built his bubble station, number 233 in the registry; his occupation now was "sculptor," and the tax people came to talk to him every year. To Julian Earth was a mudball, where ten per cent of the people lived off the labor of the other ninety percent. Oh, the brave ones shine, he told Praeger once, but the initiative that should have taken men to the stars had been ripped out of men's hearts. The whole star system was rotting, overblown with grasping things living in their own wastes. The promise of ancient myths, three thousand years old, had not been fulfilled . . .

In the watch room Praeger watched the delicate clouds which enveloped the Earth. He could feel the silence, and the slowness of the changing patterns was reassuring. Given time and left alone, the air would clean itself of all man-made wastes, the rivers would run clear again, and the oceans would regain their abundance of living things.

When his watch was over he did not wait for his relief to come. He didn't like the man. The feeling was mutual and by leaving early they could each avoid the other as much as was possible. Praeger went directly to his cubicle, lay down on his bunk, and opened the channel, both audio and visual, on the ceiling com and observation screen.

Julian's face came on promptly on the hour.

"EW-CX233 here," Julian said.

"EW-CXOO6," Praeger said. Julian looked his usual

pale self, green eyes with the look of other times still in them. "Hello, Julian. What have you been doing?"

"There was a reporter here. I made a tape of the whole thing, if you can call it an interview. Want to hear it?"

"Go ahead. My vacation was the usual. I don't know what's wrong with me."

Julian's face disappeared and the expressionless face of the reporter appeared. The face smiled just before it spoke.

"Julian—that's the name you are known by?"

"Yes."

"Will you describe your work for our viewers, Julian?"

"I am a water sculptor. I make thin plastic molds and fill them with water. Then I put them out into the void and when they solidify I go out and strip off the plastic. You can see most of my work orbiting my home."

"Isn't the use of water expensive?"

"I re-use much of it. And I am independently wealthy."

"What's the point of leaving your work outside?"

"On Earth the wind shapes rock. Here space dust shapes the ice, mutilates it, and I get the effect I want. Then I photograph the results in color, and make more permanent versions here inside."

Praeger watched Julian and the reporter float over to a large tank of water.

"Inside here," Julian said, "you see the permanent figures. When I spin the tank the density of each becomes apparent, and each takes its proper place in the suspension."

"Do you ever work with realistic subjects?"

"No."

"Do you think you could make a likeness of the Earth?"

"Why?" Praeger saw Julian smile politely. The reporter suddenly looked uncomfortable. The tape ended and Julian's face reappeared.

"See what they send up here to torment me?"

"Is the interview going to be used anywhere?" Praeger asked.

"They were vague about it."

"Have you been happy?"

Julian didn't answer. For a few moments both screens were still portraits. Both men knew all the old complaints, all the old pains. Both knew that the UN was doing secret extra-solar work, and they both knew that it was the kind of work that would revive them, just as it might give the Earth a new lease on life. But they would never have a share of it. Only a few more years of routine service, Praeger knew, and then retirement—to what? To a crowded planet.

Both men thought the same thought at that moment—the promise of space was dead, unless men moved from the solar system.

"Julian," Praeger said softly, "I'll call you after my next watch." Julian nodded and the screen turned gray.

On impulse Praeger pushed the observation button for a look at station 233. It was a steel and plastic ball one hundred feet in diameter. Praeger knew that most of Julian's belongings floated in the empty center, tied together with line. When he needed something he would bounce around the tiny universe of objects until he found it. Some parts of the station were transparent. Praeger remembered peering out once to catch sight of one of Julian's ice sculptures, and seeing a pale white ghost peer in at him for a moment before passing out of sight.

Praeger watched the silent ball that housed his friend of a lifetime. Eventually, he knew, he would join Julian in his retirement. A man could live a long time in zero-g.

The alarm in his cubicle rang and Higgins's voice came

over the audio. "That fool! Doesn't he see that orbital debris?"

Praeger had perhaps ten seconds left to see station 233 whole. The orbital junk hit hard and the air was gone into the void. The water inside, Praeger knew, had frozen instantly. Somewhere inside the ruptured body of Julian floated among his possessions even as the lights on the station winked out.

Praeger was getting into his suit, knowing there was no chance to save Julian. He made his way down the emergency passage from his cubicle, futilely dragging the spare suit behind him.

The airlock took an age to cycle. When it opened he gave a great kick with his feet and launched himself out toward the other station. Slowly it grew in front of him, until he was at the airlock. He activated the mechanism and when the locks were both open he pushed himself in toward the center of the little world.

Starlight illuminated Julian's white, ruptured face. Through the clear portion of the station Praeger saw the Earth's shadow eclipse the full Moon: a bronze shield.

For a long time after Praeger drifted in the starlit shell. He stared at the dark side of the Earth, at the cities sparkling like fireflies; never sleeping, billions living in metal caves; keeping time with the twenty-four hour workday; and where by night the mannequins danced beneath the flickering screens, their blood filled with strange potions which would give them their small share of counterfeit happiness.

Praeger tried to brush away the tears floating inside his helmet, but with no success. They would have to wait until he took his suit off. When the emergency crew arrived an hour later, he took charge.

The station was a hazard now and would have to be removed. He agreed. All this would be a funeral rite for Julian, he thought, and he was sure the artist would approve.

He removed all of Julian's written material and sent it down to his publishers, then put Julian's body in a plastic sack and secured it to the north pole of the station bubble.

He left the sculptures inside. On the body Praeger found a small note:

When we grow up we'll see the Earth not as a special place, but just as one place. Then home will be the starry cosmos. Of course this has always been the case. It is we who will have changed. I have nothing else to hope for.

The hulk continued in its orbit for three weeks, until Praeger sent a demolition crew out to it and blew it out of existence. He watched on the monitor as they set the charges that would send it into a new orbit. Station 233 would leave the solar system at an almost ninety degree angle to the plane of the ecliptic, on a parabolic path which would not bring it back to Sol for thousands of years. It would be a comet someday, Praeger thought.

He watched the charges flare up, burn for thirty seconds, and die. Slowly the bubble moved off toward the top of the screen. He watched until it disappeared from the screen. In twenty-four hours it would be beyond the boundaries of Earth. Interstellar gas and dust would scar it out of all recognition: a torn seed on the wind.

Parks of Rest and Culture

The air was foul, barely breathable, acceptable only to those who had no choice. The pool, five hundred feet long and two hundred wide, was almost completely hidden in the predawn darkness. It had once been operational, but now all the pavement was cracked and huge stones sat on the empty bottom; they had rolled down from the cliffs which rose in a semicircle at the west end of the grounds. The single granite and concrete module which had been the administration building sat on its own concrete island in the center of the waterless pool. Inside, the two floors had partially caved in. On its high granite pillar on the roof the old clock was dead at two a.m.—or p.m. The whole area had once been a park, but now the branches on the trees outside the fence were bare and brittle and dry.

Beyond the tall fence, above the dead trees, the lights from the stone city penetrated weakly through the layers of dirt-fog and morning mists. There stood the old apartment buildings which were not serviced by the numerous air filtration plants scattered throughout the city.

Praeger stood in the metal doorway of the main filter house and peered at the soft grained lights beyond the fence through his air filter mask. The face-plate sprouted a spiral hose which ended in the chemical tank strapped to his chest. At his feet he felt the vibrations of the huge pumps below ground which filtered the air, heated or cooled it for those select New York City buildings whose tenants qualified for the utility and preservice modifications under the

Human Resources Allocations Act of 1985. Such buildings had no windows, only locks at the front entrance, seldom used; each roof was a copter square.

This morning, when his night shift was over, he would have to take the subway home; the city copter was out of service. He tried to accept the thought and ignore it.

He peered up past the fence and eroded hillside through his faceplate and thought of the eyes which would be watching him as it grew lighter, when he left the grounds through the gate.

He looked to the east, where the orbital space mirror was hastening the dawn by two hours, to light up the city early with its reflected light; an effort to keep crime down. On the Asian mainland, he knew, the Russians were using similar mirrors to light up their battlefields with the Chinese.

The real dawn was more than an hour away. Praeger turned and walked back through the open doorway. He did not bother taking off his mask inside.

The plant hummed, and after a few moments the humming seemed to become a roar as the vibrating air pressed in on his ears. He walked down the row of pressure gauges, giving each one a glance. Then he went to the log pad on the wall and filled in the data. He could have done it without checking; the figures were always the same.

He went outside again as if hoping for something miraculous to happen. He stood in the open door, leaning against the metal frame and looking toward downtown—mid-Manhattan, where he could just barely see the old trade center towering over the Empire State Building, a pair of titans against the steel-gray sky. Always, he thought, the old and the new, the old never quite dying away, the dream never replacing the reality entirely. When we start for Centauri, there will still be mud huts in Asia, the unclean washing away their sins in the Ganges.

In the eastern sky an eye opened in the morning mists, a white-hot reflecting surface shouting the sun's light Earthward.

Praeger waited, and later came the true dawn; incredibly scarlet, a function of all the dirt in Earth's atmosphere, it streaked the sky. The planet could still manage its own kind of beauty. Though the wounds of the biosphere were deep, they were healing into scars. But the thin layer of human consciousness stretched over the surface of the planet—the noösphere—had ruptured; and the human organism in its entirety was being spilled back into the evolutionary past, into the abyss of screams.

In the morning sunlight the concrete surfaces of the pool area were a bright gray-white. Praeger began his walk around the fence on the inside, checking for damage; a human insect moving slowly on the slightly raised walk.

At the west end of the grounds, just below the cliffs, he found a large hole in the chain fence, the largest of six during the week. It led to the small path that ran on the other side of the fence just below the cliff wall. It was not a planned path, but one which had been created by vandals, prowlers and playing children during the years. He smiled, thinking, they have better wire cutters than the city repair crews. The hole was very neatly cut out. He turned away from the fence toward the administration building and walked briskly across.

He stopped in front of the flagpole by the front entrance, noticing that the rope had been cut again during the night. Then he went into the small office, the only usable room in the empty building, and found that the night watchman had vomited all over the floor again.

The place stank, but he forced himself to sign the blotter

and punch out on the creaky old machine. The watchman, as usual, had checked out hours ago, knowing that no one would report him, or care.

Praeger went over to the crusty old bulletin board and peered at the new addition. The examination to renew his technician's rating was to be given at 1:00 p.m., May 1, 1998, which was next Wednesday. He was worried about the rising standards and about his wife's reaction if he did not pass. Would she accept living in a non-environmental-control apartment—one open to the air, with perhaps only an air conditioner for the summer? They had adjusted well to seeing each other only in the afternoons, but she would never be—had never been—very close to him. He did not know what she would do.

He left the office and went along the walk by the fence until he came to the north exit gate, his shadow a long darkness to his right. Here once huge crowds of people had stood in line to gain entrance to the pool. He fumbled with the key and opened the rusty old lock; he pushed at the gate, straining, until it creaked open enough for him to pass. He locked it behind him and paused at the top of the stone steps which led to the street below.

Across the street stood red-brick apartment buildings, five stories each, open-windowed, unserviced by the plant in which he worked. A number of the people who lived in these buildings were hired every month during the back-blowing operation at the plant—the process by which the huge filters were removed and cleaned. Usually that was done on his shift and he supervised it with the help of two armed policemen.

He heard a clatter on the step pavement near him. A half-dozen stones struck and bounced and rolled around him. He looked up in time to see the kids on the roof of the house directly in front of him duck away from his masked gaze. He went down the steps and walked north along the street toward the Tremont subway station. He felt slightly relieved when he came to the big police cruiser parked next to a fire hydrant. Inside, the uniformed policemen were asleep in air-conditioned comfort. He stopped and rapped with his knuckles on the heavy safety plastic "glass." One of the cops woke up, looked at the dash clock, grinned and waved his thanks as Praeger turned to continue down the street. In a moment the cruiser turned on its engines and air system to high and streaked past him on its way to the precinct. As he watched it disappear ahead of him, he could almost feel the eagerness of the two cops to get to the station to check out. Momentarily he felt a keen resentment because the copter had not come to pick him up. Normally he would have been halfway home by now.

There was an old man staggering toward him down the street with one hand outstretched. "Money?" the old man said, stopping in front of him, blocking his way. The thought of the old man's mouth so near him, the mouth and nose taking in air in greedy gasps, the chest rising and falling in seeming panic, made Praeger sick. The old man's body was shaking; the effort he was exerting to control his stance resulted in a powerful sustained trembling. The eyes were bloodshot; one was set crookedly in its socket and seemed to be staring at the pavement.

Praeger shook his head. He never carried any money with him. His green city uniform would be enough to admit him to the subway.

"None left? No more—no more money?" the old man rasped in amazement. He coughed. Then his good eye also turned down to look at the pavement and he dragged himself past Praeger, as if resigned to the fact that there was nothing to be gained from this astonishing masked creature.

Praeger continued down the street. He turned the corner and went up the hill to Tremont. At the top of the hill there was a small park. Here, too, the trees were dead. There were no squirrels or birds, but a lone cockroach darted past him into the sewer. He remembered, years ago, sitting in St. James Park—on a bench, looking into the cracked and gullied clay tennis courts—watching the pigeons and squirrels moving around in the meager grass. There had even been leaves on many of the trees in those days, enough to hide the tall tower of the bank which held the Fordham clock. Then the Jerome Avenue elevated train had come by, noisier every year as the foliage diminished. It had scared the shit out of all the animals. Every year there had been more dead birds and squirrels lying around. Then, one year, there was no spring.

She came into the room and sat down on the bed where he was sleeping. "Did you hear me, Chris?" There was no urgency in her voice. He mumbled and tried to turn over but she was sitting on the covers.

"The milkman brought an extra bottle of water today by mistake, didn't you notice? I'm not going to tell him."

"Betty, let me sleep." He tried to turn over but she was still in the way. She started rubbing his stomach, to arouse him. He had been dreaming of working on a space station. . . .

He opened his eyes and looked at her. She had that usual blank look on her face, the one she wore when she wasn't angry or dreaming. Her long blond hair was combed out and she had nothing on. The daylights were on in the room. The landscape wall showed the mountain valley in Canada where she had been born. He thought of all the power she used keeping the wall on, and how little of her salary as a daycare instructor she used for the apartment.

"Betty, please get out of here and let me sleep."

"When is your exam?"

"Next Wednesday, now get out!"

She smiled and walked out of the room. The daylights and picture wall went out as she closed the door. In a moment he knew she would be dialing someone on the phone. He became drowsy again, wrapping himself in the darkness. The space station was in front of him, a jeweled toy next to a sparkling Earth.

He came into the lobby, his air mask under his left arm, and stopped under the huge glass chandelier. There was no point in worrying about the examination, he told himself. It would soon be done and over with. A large sign on the wall to his left caught his eye. He walked up to it and read the print below the huge photograph of the Earth in space. The legend urged him to take a job on one of the trans-lunar-Earth stations tied in with ecosystem and resource control.

There was a list of openings—weatherwatch, atmospheric engineering, satellite repair, orbital debris clearance. The requirements were: a technical background and aptitude, and the capacity to work alone. Benefits included generous Earth leaves, and further opportunities to work in extra-Lunar and Moon surface positions. Applications here at Central Park West Station. The wall view poster bore the name NASA-EUROSOV.

The NASA-EUROSOV office was just down the hall from the wall view poster. Praeger walked in, picked up an application from the dispenser and filled in his tech identification number. He waited a few minutes, knowing that it was now too late to get to his examination room, and dropped the computer card into the receiving slot on his way out. His tech rating could not expire before he qualified for the NASA-EUROSOV programs, which usually had to go begging for applicants.

In the hallway he thought of the disadvantages of working in space, all the little things which made it impossible for a man to do it for any great time. Physical and mental disadvantages. The Moon was better, if a man made up his mind to stay for good. Otherwise he would have to wear special weights during his stay to keep him in shape for Earthside. It was easy, they said, to put off wearing them.

He came into the lobby again and looked up at the twenty-four-hour clock on the wall. It was four in the afternoon. He had four hours before he had to be at the air plant. He went to the nearest exit which led to a sub-park shuttle and boarded a car for the museum. There he wandered around the great halls feeling somewhat lost until it was time to leave for work. He waited until the last possible moment, then put on his mask and boarded the elevator which would take him to the street lock.

There was a stillness in the waiting. The Moon was a white disk over the empty pool, riding low toward the morning. Praeger stood looking up at it through his faceplate, waiting to go off shift. Around the Moon he saw the clouds which would cover it before it set.

On the other side of the Moon, he knew, the Russians had built a grand hotel for their scientists and Moon personnel, a huge structure with gardens and fountains, where the air was very much like that of Odessa in the 1880s. It was rumored that the Russians were mining the first discovered deposits of Moon ice, and bottling some of it as a special mineral water for their more credulous countrymen. The "hotel" was really the living quarters of the large science city located in Tsiolkovsky Crater. He had heard stories of beautiful interiors, filled with red carpets and paintings, grand banquet halls and shiny brass railings, where aging Soviet leaders would go to spend their "longer years" in the one-sixth gravity. The science city itself was devoted to physics and biology and astronomy—generally to the exploitation of conditions which were unique for a variety of research programs. Even the aging bureaucrats could be made useful by entering them as case histories in various medical programs. The educated elite who lived there breathed perfect air; for them the Marxist dream of parks of rest and culture had been fulfilled; for them and those like them, technological men and scientists, would come all the fruits of knowledge, perhaps even immortality. To live on the Moon required all the planning and care which had been denied to those on Earth, and which was being given to the home world very late; but for those who had lived on the Moon for many years and would never come back, perhaps raise sons there, the bitter native land which was Earth was too beautiful in the sky to be in need of help. The American science city was less stylish, more cool and professional, but essentially the same.

On Earth one generation of the overgrown organism which was humanity would have to die off to make the population manageable again. Praeger wondered about the plague proposal made a while ago. A good plague, they had said, would leave everything standing, and mankind would have a chance to get itself back on the right path. Better than a war. Anyway, some would make it, he thought. He wondered about the long-term good of it, and the short-term evil; and the ones who would not understand, the ones who would die to create the compost for the future.

Clouds obscured the Moon and he thought, somehow . . . we men . . . were on the way to becoming fully ourselves just a little while ago, getting a grip on ourselves and reality; then we made some horrible mistake which kept us from passing that threshold into becoming something . . . new . . .

He stopped thinking and went back inside the plant to take his readings. Someday, he hoped, children would look back at this time as the great depression of the '90s . . . what year would be the cutoff point?

The apartment was quiet when he woke up that afternoon. He strained to hear Betty in the kitchen, but there was no sound. Maybe she was sitting at the table sipping coffee? He turned over and looked at her bed. It was neatly made and empty, a dark mass in the faint nightlight.

He got up slowly and stretched, went to the door, opened it, and took three strides to reach the bathroom. He found her note taped to the medicine cabinet mirror. It read: "I left you a message on the recorder." It was written in big black letters.

He turned and went out into the living room, turning the daylights on with his presence. He walked over to the green sofa and sat down, staring at the recorder on the coffee table. As he turned it on, he heard the front door open and close. He pushed the play button and looked at himself in the large mirror sitting in his pajamas. Behind him Betty came into the room.

"Chris, understand—" her voice on the tape started to say.

"Turn it off," Betty said in the mirror. He watched her in the glass. She was dressed in a green raincoat cut to look like a jacket and skirt.

"—what I'm going to tell you." He stabbed at the off button.

"I didn't want you sitting around like an orphan listening to a voice on a tape," she said. "I want to tell you myself—I owe you that much."

He wasn't going to speak to her, no matter how much he wanted to.

"I'm leaving, Chris. You're not going to make much more of yourself, you'll start to slip and we'll wind up in open housing. I'll look great when I'm wheezing and bald. I'm not going to sit around and wait for it."

He was silent, wishing she would just go.

"You're going to blame me now, aren't you?"

He shook his head suddenly, *no,* hoping that she would say it and be finished. There was a trembling in his insides. He felt as if he were in a trance which she would break with her next words.

"There's someone else and he can help me get what I want—everything we'll both ever want . . ."

He looked directly at her for a moment and saw that her lower lip was shaking. Her face was a frightening thing; it repelled him and he looked away. He began to rub his eyes with his hands. She turned and left the room. He heard the front door shut itself automatically behind her. He felt his face become drawn and he felt a great warmth surround his consciousness, as if the room were becoming a furnace; and he heard the sound of his pulse in his ears, the blood pounding behind his eyes.

It began to rain in the late afternoon and continued all night. Toward morning there were huge puddles of water in the empty pool at the air plant. The metal door to the inside jammed and Praeger had to leave it open and wear his mask all night. In the morning he took a chair and sat in the doorway watching the rain come down in the gloom, beating on the pavement. Thousands of hurrying rivulets ran on the concrete and cascaded into the empty pool. The sound of the water relaxed him. He thought of the empty apartment waiting for him, and felt the tiredness creeping into his body. He looked forward to the oblivion of sleep.

Today also the helicopter would not come for him; he was no longer worth the effort, he thought. He was leaving at the end of the week; the copter fuel was more valuable to them.

Just before he had left for work, notification had come from NASA-EUROSOV through the mail readout slot telling him they had a job for him on one of the Earth-Moon sector stations. He was to settle his affairs and vacate his apartment. There had been a word of congratulations on the print-out, and a note asking him if he would waive minimum Earth leave for higher pay.

As a NASA-EUROSOV employee he had regained the right to have children, indirectly, by depositing his sperm; a right which Betty had convinced him to sell. But the sperm bank was a good bet against the future. He had heard of illegal children being readied for a new Earth swept clean by deliberate plague; children hidden away throughout the solar system. Somewhere, he was sure, men were preparing for the stars. He dreamed of unspoiled Earths around far suns, wondering how long it would be before the stardrive breakthrough changed the world and if he would be part of it.

He went off shift and walked up the hill to the Tremont station. The rain ran down his Pyrex faceplate. He wore no hat and his hair was wet. His clothing was waterproof. He tightened his collar to keep the water from running inside. The rain seemed to be coming down harder than before and he could not see very far ahead. He needed a windshield wiper, like the big blades on the police cruiser. The thought tickled him—sweep, sweep! He couldn't see it but he could feel it: the water was high around his boots as it ran down the hill.

Two men grabbed his arms and twisted them behind his back and a third ripped off his air mask, chest tank and all. They pushed him on his back with his head downhill and in a moment they vanished again in the thick curtain of rain.

He got up breathing hard and coughing. The air was heavy and wet in his lungs and he felt nauseated. His wrists seemed sprained. His face was streaming. Water ran in his eyes, blinding him. He screamed and shook both his fists in the rain; the gesture hurt, and the sound was lost against the rush of water in his ears. His eyes began to hurt and he rubbed them, cursing silently now. Then he walked the remaining half block to the subway entrance, coughing without letup all the way.

The entrance was a gaping black hole leading down into the Earth, surrounded by a wilderness of rain. On the platform he took out a handkerchief and tied it around his face.

On the train going uptown he knew the other passengers were all staring at him, secretly pleased that he had lost his mask; but when he confronted their eyes they seemed to lose interest in him. He wondered, did NASA-EUROSOV know about Betty leaving him? Was that why they had mentioned the e-visitation clause, knowing that he would have no immediate ties on Earth? If she had started the divorce action, then central information—CENTIN—would have it in his file, which could have been already tapped by NASA-EUROSOV. He could check it, but it didn't really matter.

The sperm deposit. That, too. If he had gone in to be sterilized, they would have given him money, just like for blood, just like they had sold their right to have kids. But now they would put his sperm in a bank, with the eventual certainty that it would be used. Someone was making all possible bets against the future, making sure that as many different combinations were at least available as possible. He was sure that it was being used as a kind of incentive to go along with his new job.

He thought of the stories he had heard of hidden groups of children belonging to high officials on Earth or on the Moon, children being readied for a new Earth, maybe even the stars? He hoped, perhaps something will happen and we'll get a stardrive in my lifetime, and if I'm out there working when it happens maybe I'll get in on it! He felt a wild surge of expectation at the thought, a momentary release from the dark prison of his puny self.

The train reached his station and delivered him into the drenching rain and acrid air, again.

At the end of the week he closed the apartment and took a jet to Nevada, where the whip catapult serving the Earth stations was located. The desert conjured up visions of the sun domes on Mars, green plants growing lush in low gravity, filling the bright space of the dome with oxygen. He did not have to wear a mask here, in Nevada, where the helicopter had left him off. What of Mars, where the desert bloomed . . . what of Earthlike planets around far suns, unspoiled! How soon, he wondered, will we make the crucial breakthrough which will save us—tip the balance in favor of our dreams? A gust of wind came up from nowhere and blew some sand in his face and made his eyes water.

The spaceport was surrounded by a city of trailers and

cabins. They gave him a cabin with a skylight for the one day before his departure for Earth Station One. He lay resting, and then dreaming, in the stillness of half sleep, of sun over treetops, an uncancerous sun, setting; a sliver of daylight Moon; sky deep blue; evening star blazing; wind on the tall grass; shadows of clouds; last spring with no sound in the air . . .

The last real spring he had known had been in Central Park, years ago. The water of the small lake had been a green mirror, and the white swan had sailed curve-necked toward where the willows washed their branches in the water . . .

Tomorrow he would be on the shuttle.

The Earth was blue-green below as he recalled yesterday's thought of being here now. Acceleration was over and he leaned weightless in his straps toward the porthole, knowing that the stars and Moon would look clearer now than from Earth, that bottom of a dirty ocean where he had been born. It was a clean break now. Sunlight flooded the shuttlecraft like a shout. He floated back in his seat and tightened the straps, and dreamed of a healed Earth as it might still be, one hundred . . . five hundred . . . years hence, free of its billions and the guilty minority responsible for a century of plunder.

He dreamed he saw parks of rest and culture filled with elegant people, full-leafed trees casting broad shadows; and at night stars would be looking down, bright lights in an empty hall above an Earth abandoned by most of its people.

Assassins of Air

Gloom concealed the city, an obscurity born of dying night and pollutants hanging motionless in the air, a massive shadowy stillness pressing down on the pavement, billions of particles ready to swirl through the stone alleys with the morning wind. Praeger squatted by the iron fence in the alleyway, waiting for Uruba and Blue Chip to come back. He looked at his watch and saw it was one hour to dawn, and he would have to leave if they didn't return before then.

Suddenly he heard them creep into the alley. They knew where he was and came to squat near him by the fence.

"How many, Chris?" Uruba asked.

"Twenty real old ones," Christian Praeger said.

"Hey, kid, Uruba and me broke off forty-one pieces of chrome," Blue Chip said.

"Don't knock him," Uruba said, "Chris here is only nineteen, just startin' out. One fine day he'll run his own recycling gang, when we's all rich. He'll feed the junkman all the old cars on the East Coast, kill them all, help make the air cool and clean again." Uruba coughed. "Got it stashed all ready to be picked?"

Praeger nodded. It was almost light enough in the alley for him to see Uruba's black face and the gray scar on his cheek.

"I'll slap the bread on you tomorrow, Chris," Uruba said. He clapped Praeger on the shoulder and started to get up.

"I need it now," Praeger mumbled. "I have to pay for my

PLATO lessons. I gotta have it, honest."

Uruba was standing looking down at him now, and Blue Chip stood up next to him. "I have to," Praeger said as he stood up with them.

Uruba hesitated, almost as if the request had been a personal insult. Then he smiled. "Sure, kid, how much?"

"Twenty-five," Praeger said.

The smile disappeared, but he counted out the money. "This one time, kid. Next time you wait like all the other dudes. I pay off, my word is good, right?"

Praeger nodded meekly. He folded the bills into his jeans pocket, trying not to look at their faces. But Uruba and Blue Chip turned from him and walked out of the alley, and he was relieved by the fact that he would not see them for at least two weeks.

He looked at his watch. It would be completely light in less than a half hour. He sprinted out of the alley and up the gray-lighted street toward the subway at 145th Street. He started coughing and slowed his pace to a walk to cut down his need for air.

PLATO, the sign read: PROGRAMMING LOGIC FOR AUTOMATIC TEACHING OPERATIONS. Once the facility had been free, just like chest X-rays. Now students had to pay to milk the machine, twenty dollars a rap, but it was a good teach if you wanted to learn a skill.

Praeger went up the wide steps leading into the library and paid his money at the ticket booth. An usher showed him to his usual booth in the big research hall.

The program was teaching him the workings of the city air filtration system, which was fully operational in Manhattan and slowly expanding. He knew that many technical dudes would be needed to service and maintain it, and he was going to be in on it after he finished clouting cars. The old cars were paying for his lessons, but next year, or the year after, they would be gone—leaving only the safety-cars, public wheels and the electric push to rush people around.

The new electric cars weren't bad, but there was something in the older people that loved the rush of power. So the old vehicles were slow in going, especially with all the bootleg mechanics servicing them to keep them legal. The old wheels were assassinating the atmosphere, Uruba said. We kill them, recycle the people's resources and make some bread on the deal, too. Uruba was right, Praeger thought; he would not have his PLATO lessons without that money. Only Uruba did a lot of other things in the city, like running a supply of young girls to the insular estates outside. Uruba did not care about being right. It was a coincidence, sometimes.

Praeger put on his earphones. The first exam question appeared on the screen and he answered it correctly.

When he came out of the library at two in the afternoon, he saw the old '74 station wagon growling down Fifth Avenue spewing blue smoke from its tail pipe. It was a contrast to the bulky crashproof Wankels, steamers and slow electrics moving on the street with it. He watched it stop and park near the corner of 42nd Street. The car was only ten years old, so its owner could still get away with it by claiming that it hadn't fallen apart. He could keep running it legally until it did, but even with its filters it was a polluter. Maybe the owner wasn't even having it fixed on the side, Praeger thought; maybe it still ran well. As he stood at the top of the stairs, he hated the dirty wheels, hated them as he would a fearful beast that had somehow gotten loose in the world of men.

He waited until the owner left the car, then went to where it was parked and lifted the hood, took out his pocket tool and began removing the spark plugs. That done, he cut a few wires with his pocketknife. He closed the hood quickly and walked away from the car. No one had noticed him. Later tonight someone would strip it down for all of its valuables, Uruba or one of the other gangs. Another one of the old killers was effectively dead. He thought of his dead parents as he slipped the spark plugs into the sewer drain at the corner.

Praeger stood on the roof of his apartment building looking up at the stars hiding on the other side of the air; still, the brighter ones were clearly visible, drawing him away from the Earth to the brightly lit space stations circling the planet and out to the diamondlike Moon domes where men seemed to be doing something worthwhile. He saw Uruba and Blue Chip living in the shadows of the universe, profiting from changes that would happen without them. He thought of the White Assassins, Savage Skulls, Black Warlocks and Conservative Angels—all the night rulers of New York City. He thought of their words, political phrases copied after the Black Lords and Young Panthers, the largest national groups. He thought of his PLATO lessons, which would liberate him from his open-air-intake apartment, take him away from the memory of his parents and public schooling, give him something to do in which he could take pride.

He was going to do something else, and soon. In two weeks, he estimated, he would be ready to take the computer tests for a technical rating. He would have to tell Uruba and Blue Chip that he wanted out, but he wasn't sure how he would say it to them.

He turned around and went down the stairs to his apartment.

Uruba squinted at him in the dim light of the basement room. Blue Chip had gone to get a bulb for the shaded light hanging darkly over the old card table where they were sitting.

"You cost me money, man. Why you going to quit?"

Blue Chip came back with a bulb and screwed it into the socket. The lamp swung back and forth for a moment and stopped when Uruba pulled the switch cord. Yellow light filled the dusty cellar room.

"Yellow's all I could find," Blue Chip said.

Praeger looked at Uruba. His black face looked strange in the light. Uruba smiled at him grotesquely, showing him his one gold tooth.

"Chris here wants out," Uruba said. "What do you think, Blue Chip?"

Blue Chip giggled nervously and leaned his chair back on its hind legs.

"I know," Blue Chip said, "he's been going to school on the sly to them PLATO lessons."

Uruba grinned. "You tryin' to be better than us, is that right?" he asked. And he left a big silence for Praeger to drown in.

Finally he answered. "I just want other kinds of things, that's all," he said.

"The honko always goes back," Blue Chip said. "How much have you stashed?"

"Where you going, Chris, to the Moon resorts with all the rich cats?" asked Uruba. "Where's all your bread? Have you been cheating on us?"

"I just want a tech rating to work in the new air plants.

The money's good," Praeger said.

Uruba leaned forward and knocked the card table into the air, breaking the yellow light. "What the rest of us going to breathe?" he asked in the darkness. "Who you think can move into those air-control apartments? Chris, you're a fool."

"Things may get better," Praeger managed to say.

"Like hell," Blue Chip announced from a dark corner of the room. The only light in the room now came in through the small window near the door.

Praeger went to the door quickly, opened it and ran up the old steps to the street. He was out of breath when he reached the sidewalk. He stopped, and from below he heard the sound of Uruba's laughter, mocking his fear.

It stopped. Then Uruba screamed after him from below the pavement. "Chris, I helped you, I got you started, I taught you, boy—and this is what I get? I'm gonna get you, man. You better hide your money, you hear!" The voice died away, and Praeger stood perfectly still in front of the old brownstone. Then he was shaking and his body was covered with sweat. He looked up at the sky, at all the old buildings in this sealed-off part of old Harlem. He looked downtown where the light construction on New York's second level looked like a huge diamond-studded spider devouring the city in the night. Slowly, he began walking home.

Eyes watched him when he went to his PLATO lessons and when he came home. On Tuesdays and Thursdays when he stayed home he felt them on the windows of his fifth-floor apartment on 10th Street, and he was afraid to go near the windows; but when he tried to see if anyone was following him, he could find no one.

In the middle of the night on a Monday a crash of glass woke him in bed. He got up and went into the living room, turning on the light. He saw a large rock lying on the floor, then checked the front-door police lock. It was still firm. Then he got some cardboard and tape from the kitchen and began taping up the broken window.

As he worked he told himself that he understood all this. Uruba wanted one thing: to rend and tear and hurt him. He was an easy target, easier to hurt than the cops in their air-conditioned tank cars, easier to destroy than a car. And to hurt him meant more than money, that's how Uruba was thinking. Praeger was a deserter, and Uruba could not accept that. For Blue Chip it was recreation to hound him, and Blue Chip also thought Praeger was hiding money.

He had just put a final piece of tape on the window when two shots came through the cardboard. Praeger fell to the floor and lay still. He lay there for an hour, afraid to move. Finally he crawled behind the sofa, where he fell into a nervous sleep just before morning.

He was going to have to leave town. Uruba was crazy and it would get worse. His exams and PLATO would have to wait.

He packed a knapsack and went down into the basement, where he kept his old motorcycle. He wheeled it out into the yard, which was connected to the street by a concrete ramp. He looked at his watch. The glowing numbers told him it was an hour to dawn.

He started the bike with a shove of his foot and rolled down the ramp slowly. He turned into the street and started in the direction of Riverside Drive. The streets were deserted at this hour.

After a few minutes he noticed the lights of the car behind him. He gunned the bike and shot up the entrance to Riverside and out onto the highway. Traffic was light and he continued accelerating.

A few minutes later the car was still behind him and gaining. To his left the river was covered by fog, but the lights on the Jersey shore were coming through. Praeger gunned his engine and the bike carried him forward, past two Wankel safety-tanks moving slowly to their destination. He looked at his speedometer and saw that he was doing 115. He knew that the new-looking car behind him could catch him, but he had a head start. He thought, I have a right to try to better myself, go to school. The money came from Uruba's world, he knew that, but there was no other way. Food was given out free, just enough, but more than that could be bought only with skills. You could go to school if you paid for it, but you could live without it. It was a luxury for those who had a hunger for it. Uruba hated him for wanting it.

As he rushed through the night, Praeger felt tears in his eyes blurring the highway and the sight of the river with its lights on the far shore. The air was damp on his face, and the road was an unyielding hardness under the bike's rubber wheels.

The car was still in his mirror, its lights on bright to annoy him. It was winding its way past the occasional electrics and steamers on the road, coming closer. He pushed forward on the black road, trying to move beyond the light beams on his back.

The car disappeared from his mirror. Praeger accelerated, eager to press his momentary advantage. He had the road to himself for the next few minutes. Then the road curved upward and to the right, and he was rushing over the small bridge into the Bronx. He saw the car in his mirror again when he took the Grand Concourse entrance, and it kept pace with him along the entire six miles of the wide avenue. Ten minutes later he was on the edges of the old city, fleeing upstate.

Here he was among the dying trees northwest of New York, dark outlines against the night sky, thousands of acres of lifeless woodland, a buckled carpet of hills and gullies. He had taken the old two-way asphalt roadway in the hope of losing Uruba's shiny antique.

Praeger felt a strange sensation on the back of his neck when he saw the car in his mirror again. It wasn't Uruba following him in the car, hating him; it was the car, fixing him with its burning eyes, ready to come forward and crush him under its wheels. The car was trying to hold him back, getting even for all of its kind he had killed with Uruba. It was trying to stop him from escaping to another kind of life, just as it had stopped his parents. The car hated the soft creatures living in the world with it, hated the parasites who were slowly taking away its weapons, taming it, making it an unpoisonous and powerless domestic vehicle.

Around him in the night stood the naked trees, the stripped victims of the car's excretions. He listened to the thick drone of the motorcycle engine. He was riding a powered insect that was brother to the wheeled beast pursuing it, jaw open to swallow. The Moon brushed out from behind the thinning clouds on his left, riding low over the trees, its white light frighteningly pale.

He went around a wide curve in the road, holding closely to the right shoulder, momentarily escaping the car's lights. He came out into a short straightaway and suddenly the road curved again, and the car was still out of sight behind him.

He gunned the engine to the limit, hoping to stay ahead for good.

Suddenly his headlight failed, leaving him to rush forward alone in the darkness. The Moon slid behind some clouds. There was some kind of small bridge ahead. He had glimpsed it in the Moonlight; now he could barely see its latticework against the sky. In a moment he knew what he was going to do. He braked the cycle and jumped at the last moment.

He hit the road shoulder and rolled to a stop. The bike rushed over the bridge to the other side and into some trees, where it stopped with a crunch.

Praeger saw that he was lying near an old roadblock horse that had a detour sign nailed to it. He got up and dragged it to block the road to the bridge and to direct traffic to the right, directly onto the slope that ran down to the river.

He sprinted into the deadwood forest and hid behind a tree. In a moment he heard Uruba's wheels screeching in the turns. The headlights came around the bend, ghostly rays cutting through the darkness. There was not time for the car to do anything but follow the detour arrow. He heard the brakes go on but it was too late. The left headlight shattered against the roadblock and the car flew over the edge, turning over on its front end when it hit bottom and landing in the river top down.

It burst into a fireball and burned in its own bleedings, which set the river on fire, the dark-flowing river filled with sludge and acid and slaughterhouse blood, flammable chemicals and the vitals of all Earth's creatures. The fire spread quickly under the bridge, and the old wooden structure started to catch fire.

Praeger left his hiding place and ran across the bridge, hoping to find his cycle in working order. The stench from the river was enough to make him gasp as he went across. From the other side he looked down at the burning hulk, a dark beast engulfed by flames, and the river, which would burn up- and downstream until the fire reached areas free of flammable materials.

Praeger sat down on the far bank and watched the burning. It wasn't Uruba who was dying, not just Uruba or Blue Chip. It was a creature dying there in the dirty waters—the same waters that a few years ago had threatened the East with a new pollution-fed microorganismic plague. For a few months it had looked as if a new killer, much like bubonic plague, would be loosed on the land; fortunately by that time many rivers could be burned, or easily helped to catch fire, and the threat of epidemic had passed away in a cleansing flame.

Uruba had been a scavenger living off the just laws and man's efforts to reclaim nature for himself. Praeger felt as if he were coming out of a strange confusion, a living dream that had held him in its grasp. A slight wind blew the stifling fumes from the river toward him, making his eyes water, oppressing him with a sadness too settled for tears, even though they were present on his face.

Later the flames died to a flicker on the waters. The sky cleared in the east and the morning star came out, brilliant before the sun, still hiding below the horizon. As the sun came up, Praeger could see the towers of the city to the south, their glassy facets catching the sun's shout.

He got up and looked around at the stricken forest land in the morning light, patched here and there with new greenery struggling out of the ground and along tree branches. The bridge at his right was a cinder, still slowly collapsing into the river. He decided to make his way along the bank on foot until he found another bridge where he could cross to the other side and return to the city.

The Soft Terrible Music

Each of Castle Silverstone's one hundred windows looked out on the landscape of a different country.

The iron drawbridge opened on Mars.

A stainless steel side gate led out into a neighborhood in Luna City. A small bronze gate opened in a small public place aboard Odalisque, the largest of the Venusian floating islands drifting high above the hot, dry desert of the planet.

A sliding double door opened through the sheer face of a cliff overlooking Rio de Janiero, where one could stand before an uncrossable threshold.

There was also a door that led nowhere. It was no different in function than the other doors, except that it was not set to any destination. This castle, like any true home, was the expression of a man's insides, desolate places included.

When the castle was not powered-up for full extension, it stood on a rocky hillside in Antarctica's single warm valley, where it had been built in the early twenty-second century by Wolfgang Silverstone, who rented it out occasionally for political summits. In design it was a bouquet of tall, gleaming cylinders, topped with turrets from a variety of castle building periods. The cylinders surrounded a central courtyard, and the brief connecting walls were faced with gray stone that had been quarried from the valley.

The castle got its name as much from the flecks of fool's silver in the stone as from the name of its builder. The castle also differed from other extended homes, because it was not linked to the houses of friends and relatives, or to apartments and pieds-à-terre in major cities. The castle had its vistas, and one could step out into them, but its exits were private. Some of them even looped back into chambers within the castle.

Few homes had ever been built with as much care and attention to a human being's future needs, to his own future failings. Deep within himself, Silverstone knew what would happen, had accepted it, and had made provisions for his fate.

Halfway through construction, he altered some of the keep's plans to attract a single woman—Gailla, the woman with the perfect memory, who by age eighty had read and retained every novel written since the eighteenth century. Silverstone, in a fit of fibbing, told her that his castle had a library of one thousand previously lost and unknown works, that he found her irresistible, and that if she married him for the minimum allowable term he would give her the key to the library.

As he waited for Gailla's answer, his nights trembled with odd dreams, in which he felt that he had always known her, even though he was certain that they had never met—at least not physically. Upon waking, he would conclude that he must have seen her image somewhere; or, more simply, that he wanted her so desperately that his unconscious was inventing an unbroken history of romance, to convince him that they had always been together in their love.

What was five years of a term marriage, he told her; another century of life waited. He was not unattractive for a child of fifty, even if he said so himself. The prize of books he offered seemed to draw her curiosity. Its very existence intrigued her. But secret libraries were not unknown. The Vatican still had much of one locked away, and the history of the Middle East and North Africa was filled with stories of vanished libraries waiting under the sands along ancient, dried-up waterways. One more lost library was not an impossibility.

Fearful that she would leave him if he did not make good on his original boast, he told her that his treasure was a library of books that had been saved from the great "paper loss" of 1850–2050, when most acid paper books had crumbled to dust because there had been no money or will to preserve them; the world had been too busy dealing with global warming and rising ocean levels. He had found the books on his forays into various abandoned Antarctic bases, where the dry cold had preserved the paper. They were mostly mysteries, science fiction, adventure, suspense, bestsellers, and romance novels brought by the base personnel for amusement. Only about a thousand volumes.

As it turned out, she soon discovered that the books were a fraud. Silverstone confessed that he had found only a few; the rest were written to complete extant scraps, cover designs and jacket blurbs, by paid specialists who did not know for whom they were working or that they were part of a larger effort. But fraud or not, it was at least an echo of a newly discovered library, and given enough time, it would become interesting in itself, he assured her, and it seemed to him that she appreciated the compliment of his ploy.

He told her how paper had been made and aged, covers painted, fingerprints of the dead scattered through the volumes. Gailla seemed delighted—for about a month—until she saw how bad the books were, how trite and poorly written. Silverstone was delighted by her bedroom habits—also for about a month. She lost interest in him at about the same time she was able to prove that the books, from internal anachronisms, were fakes.

"How dare you!" she screamed, careful to put on a convincing show. "Why did you do it?"

"To attract you," he answered, astonished by her perfectly controlled bitterness, which seemed to hide another purpose. "Are you sorry? Would you have bonded with me for myself?"

"You never gave me the chance!" she sang out in a voice that began as a low grumble and ended in a high soprano.

"But you would have," he demanded, "in other circumstances?"

The question seemed to upset her greatly, and she gave no answer; but Silverstone was convinced that she was holding back a no, and he began to wonder why he had ever been attracted to her. It had seemed to him at the beginning that she would alter the course of his life, change the unknown fate that lay hidden in the back of his mind; and now it seemed to him that nothing could save him from it. It was as if she had known all along about the abyss that threatened to open before him, and was waiting for the right moment to push him into it—after she had tormented him with doubt for a sufficient period of time.

He often went to one window after another, as if looking for a landscape into which he might disappear. Autumn scenes drew him, especially mountainous ones with streams, where the leaves on the trees were turning gold and brown. Then he hungered for the sterility of desert sands; and this gave way to a need for lush jungles, and then windswept plains. He became insatiable, passing from window to window like a thief in a museum, eyeing the views greedily, feeling that there could never be enough windows.

Sometimes he liked to step out on Mars, onto his small

patch of it, where he could stand and marvel at the honeycomb of habitats spreading across the planet. Five-sided, one thousand-foot-high transparent cells, immediately habitable in the Martian sunlight—they would one day roof over the red planet with an indoor-outdoors, thus solving the problem of keeping a permanent atmosphere on a low-gravity world. Here was an achievement he envied, wishing that he had been its architect. It was an accomplishment in the making that no amount of inherited wealth could buy.

There were afternoons when he would slip through the gate into Luna City and wander through the VR-game bazaars, where the miners bought their cruel distractions.

Passing into his small hotel room on Odalisque, the Venusian floating island, he would shower and dress for dinner at the Ishtar Restaurant, where huge wall-screens revealed a radar imaging of the bleak landscape fifty kilometers below, which waited for human ambitions to make a mark on it.

And at least once a month he would stand in the alcove above Rio and stare out at the city below as if it were his hometown, imagining the old streets as if he had once known them.

And again, as with the windows, there were not enough doors to satisfy him. Every *there* became a *here* when he came to it, losing the longing-magic that drew him.

On the battlements at night, as he considered his deteriorating situation with Gailla, it was—the stars! the stars!—that gave him any kind of peace. By day he felt exposed to the sky, whether a white sheet of overcast or the brilliant glare of yellow sun in a deep blue sky. In the evenings, when he took a short walk across the bare valley of stone, it was always a walk across himself, in search of something he had lost. When he stopped and looked back at the castle, he felt that he had left himself behind. Returning, he felt better, except that Gailla was still there, an intruder deep within him, and he regretted bitterly ever having let her in.

Trying to think how he might extricate himself, he would visit the castle's dungeons, where the heat exchangers drew strength from the hot springs beneath the bedrock to run the electric generators. Here, also, were the brightly lit hothouses that grew his flowers and vegetables. He did not feel exposed beneath this well-defined, contained, and nourishing daylight. Sitting there, watching the vegetables grow, he calmed himself enough to think that he would simply let the minimum term of his marriage run out. There was only a year and a half left. That would be the simplest solution. Until then, he would simply keep out of her way.

But asleep in his own room, he would often hear her moving inside him, opening doors and closing them, as if looking for something. He would wake up and hear her doing the same thing again, and he wondered what she had come into him to find. And he realized, although some part of him had known it all along, that there were two castles, that there had been two castles from the very moment he had conceived the plans for its construction in this valley—one castle outside and one within himself, and that Gailla had invaded both of them.

He began to wonder what she was looking for, and decided that he would have to spy on her to find out. Had she married him to steal something? What did he have that required so much effort? If it was so desirable, maybe he should also know about this prize, and prevent her from stealing it. What could it be? He already had everything that money could buy.

During the night of January 31st, he slept lightly, and when he heard her opening and closing doors, he got up and dressed, then went out to see what he could learn. He found her on the second level of the north turret, going from room to room down the spiral staircase, opening every door, shining a light inside, then backing away and leaving the door slightly ajar. He listened to her from behind a Freas tapestry, until she reached the bottom. There she sighed as if greatly satisfied, and went down the final curve of the stairway into the main hall below.

He crept out from his hiding place and hurried to the railing, from which he looked down and saw her pacing before the great fireplace, where the dying embers of a collapsed universe still glowed. She was dressed in her outdoor jumpsuit, but it could not conceal her tall, slender shape. At last she sat down in one of the great high chairs and closed her eyes in contentment.

It made no sense at all.

"You can come down, Wolfy," she called out suddenly. "I know you're there!"

Was she bluffing, he wondered. Had she called out like this on several nights, out of a general suspicion?

She looked up suddenly and pointed to where he stood. "I can't quite see you in this wretched light, but you're there in the shadow near the railing."

She was not bluffing. He leaned over and said, "I'll be right with you," then came down the stairs, hoping that now he would at last learn what she was after, crossed the hall, and sat down in the high-backed chair facing hers.

Staring at her intently, he was about to ask what she was looking for.

"Be patient," she said, expecting his question.

He looked at her, puzzled. "And you bonded with me just to . . . carry on some kind of search? Whatever for?"

"You'll know soon enough, Wolfy."

"Do you even know yourself?"

"I know," she said, and as the redness of the embers painted her face, it seemed that she was about to become someone else.

"So tell me," he said. "It's something I'll have to know sooner or later—right?"

She nodded grimly and said, "More than you want to know. But before I tell you, Wolfy, be advised that people know where I am."

"What do you think I'll do to you?" he asked with surprise.

"Let me tell you a story . . ."

He settled back in his chair.

"During the plague deaths of the twenty-first century," she began, "a man was born in Rio. He grew up to be a thief, a murderer, a crooked politician, a mayor of more than one city, and finally the president of a country. In a depopulated world, his talents were needed, and he did well in administrative posts, although always to his own benefit. But as the century grew old and the population began to increase again, people became more jealous of political and economic power, and sought to take back from him what he had gained. He defended himself, of course, but when he saw that he would be brought down, either by assassination or by imprisonment, he decided that he had to die. So he went to a rich friend who was a recluse, killed him, and then stepped into the man's identity, through somatic changes of his own physique, which already resembled that of the victim, and finally through selective memory implants. And then he went one step further, desperate to cover his trail completely. He wiped away his own self to prevent capture, and became Wolfgang Silverstone, as completely as anyone could, short of having actually been Wolfgang Silverstone."

"What!" Silverstone cried out.

"Sit down and calm yourself, Wolfy. You can't know right now that any of this is true, but trust me, the trail is still there, because you didn't want to hide it completely."

"That's crazy. It's the same as suicide!"

"No, the man from Rio planned to come back."

"What?"

"Yes, he left a 'trigger' inside his stolen persona, so that one day it would resurrect his earlier self. I'm certain of that. This trigger is what I've been looking for. It's here in this castle, and even you don't know where it is, even though you had it built as part of your way back. The man you were was too egotistical to have allowed himself to become someone else permanently. You're not the man you were, but you will be, very soon now."

Silverstone laughed. "But how?"

"There's a pre-trigger," she said, "that will guide you to the place at the appropriate time, and there you will know how to free your true self and become again the man who killed the original Silverstone." She recited the words softly, as if she had rehearsed them a thousand times—which, of course, she had.

Silverstone stood up and lurched toward her, but she pointed a weapon at him wearily and said, "Sit down, Wolfy. Do you think I would have told you all this without some insurance?"

He stopped, then stumbled back into his chair. "Who are you?" he asked. "What is all this to you?"

She shrugged. "Police—and there's no statute of limitations on murder."

He sat back, stunned. "But surely you see . . . that you have no proof beyond this story you've told me. You personally don't know that it's true. You're just putting bits and pieces together."

"You've been getting restless lately," she said, "as if you were looking for something—and you have been, constantly. You're getting close to the time you set for triggering your own return. You see, even in your persona state, your guilt remains, buried deeply, of course. Even your building this castle is part of that. You built it as a way of exploring yourself, of setting the means for your return. You'll give me all the proof I need, because you'll go to a certain prepared room at the appointed time and come out guilty of murder. It's why I'm here, and why I married you."

He laughed. "But I can't know that any of this is true!" he shouted. "Even you admit that. If I don't go to this room, you'll have no case. Even if I do go in, I don't have to say anything when I come out. Why did you bother to tell me all this? You might have done better leaving me in the dark. Mind you, that's still assuming any of this is true."

"I want you to suffer for a while."

"Did you find the room? You certainly spent enough nights annoying me with your explorations."

"Shut up, Wolfy. You're just a clever sociopath living through a dead man's memories. You set up a time for retrieving yourself, after stealing from people in troubled times. I suppose even a thug wants to be himself, to come back from, in effect, being dead."

"How long must a man lie dead," he recited, puzzled by the words that came out of him. "Forever is too long. There must be mercy somewhere."

"See, you're in there, all right," she replied, "speaking out even though you don't quite know it."

Shaken, he asked derisively, "Did you call him Wolfy?

And were you his she-wolf?"

"Shut up!"

"You'll never call anyone but me Wolfy again," he said. "What can getting this other guy bring you?"

"He'll be at peace. I'll be at peace, knowing that the murderer of my beloved has been exposed."

"Oh, then you won't kill me yourself? You'll just have them take me away."

"But first you'll have to live again as the man you were."

He sat slightly forward in his chair and her hand tensed around her gun. "But don't you see," he said earnestly. "I'm not responsible. I know only what you've told me about all this. I don't know or feel anything about the crime."

"Don't worry, it'll all come back to you. That's why you did it this way, so you could say that you weren't responsible. It's part of your crime."

"Really?"

"You set it up, and I've caught you."

"Are you sure? Beware, you may not like what you find."

"Don't threaten me," she said. "You are Benito Alonso Robles, the man from Rio, who killed Wolfgang Silverstone in 2049 and downloaded the essentials of his personality into your own, overwriting yourself for a timed period in order to evade the police. Murder was only your last crime, designed to conceal all the others. We can't get you on many of those, but we will certainly get you for murder."

"How clever of me," Silverstone said. "So what now?"

She did not answer him.

"Consider," he continued, "that if I am all that is left of Silverstone, your so-called beloved, then why didn't I remember you when we met?"

"We were no longer together when you killed him," she

said, "and sometime before that, in order to ease his pain, he had suppressed his experiences with me. Still, I think something in you seemed to know me."

"Ah! And then I fell in love with you again. That was why I was so earnest, so eager. But how could I know, my dear?" He held his arms out to her. "And now you want to destroy all that survives of your beloved, even after what was left of him was strong enough to come after you again!"

"No—you're only a fragment of him, and you've developed in ways he would not have, had he lived. For one thing, there's a different unconscious below the superimposed personality and its memories, and that makes you very different."

"Still, I'm all that's left of Wolfy dearest."

"But not any part that knows me very well," she said coldly. "Why did you pick him? Had he done you any wrong?"

"How do I know? If all this is true, then he was simply convenient, I suppose. Ask me later—if we get to later, and if any of this is true."

"Get up," she said. "We're going upstairs."

"Is it time, my dearest?"

"I don't know. Do you feel anything? You may have already spoken the pre-trigger."

He stood up and she motioned for him to climb the great stairs to the second level of the north tower. As he started up, she followed well below him, gun aimed at his back.

"Keep going," she said when he reached the landing.

"How do you know it's up here?" he asked.

"Where would you say, then?"

"The lower levels?" he said, laughing. "How would I know? If what you say is true, I may even be the man you say I killed—I mean physically as well as whatever identity was fed in."

"You're not," she said. "I've already had your DNA checked."

He laughed again. "Of course, the opportunity presented itself to you on more than one occasion. You simply carried a sample away in you." He turned around and faced her with open hands. "Gailla," he said, "you don't know what you're doing and neither do I, by your own claims. You don't know how the pre-trigger will kick in, or where this . . . this restoration will take place. And you admit that as far as I know, I am Silverstone . . ."

"You're not him," she said. "That much I know."

"Yes, yes, the DNA. But I only have your word for that too."

"Do you feel anything?" she asked. "An impulse to go somewhere, or say something to yourself?"

"Not particularly."

"Just a few moments ago you wanted to go to the lower levels below the castle."

"An idle remark."

"It might mean something."

"Well, I have lived with a vague expectation of some kind for a while now. It came to me just after we . . . no longer got along."

"Really."

"Maybe your being a cop spooked me at some basic level." He turned around suddenly and watched her tense. He waited a moment, then asked, "What do you really want from me? Simple revenge, is that it?"

"No, I just want you to know again, consciously, what you did, and let the law do with you as it will. That's revenge enough."

"But what if I never remember?"

"That's what we're here for," she said. "You took him from me a long time ago, and denied us a chance of ever getting back to each other. We might have by now."

"It's pretty to think so, and sad that you do."

"You don't really care."

"Not much. You're purging me of any desire I once had for you."

"Sorry I can't say the same. It was never there."

"Are you sure?"

"Turn around and get going."

He smiled, turned, and climbed the spiral.

"Stop right there," she said suddenly. "Face the door on your right."

He obeyed. "Why here?"

"Process of elimination," she said. "You have never entered this room since we've been together. Do you recall ever entering it?"

"As a matter of fact, I don't."

"Go in."

He pressed his palm to the plate, and the door slid open. He stepped inside. She came in right behind him. The door slid shut. An overhead panel of light blinked on, filling the room with bright yellow light, and he saw another door at the end of the room.

Then he looked to his right and saw the portrait on the wall.

He turned and gazed up at a dark painting of someone sitting at a mahogany desk. It was an old man with thin white hair teased out to twice the size of his head. He was dressed in a bright red nineteenth century military tunic that seemed to be choking his wrinkled neck. There were no markings on the tunic to indicate nationality. The man's mouth was closed tightly. . . .

And as he stared at the face, a flood of returning memory filled his mind, and he knew that this was the trigger. And with his memories came also the remembrance of the day he had set the trigger at the portrait of Silverstone's ancestor. Then, packed away, the painting had waited for the castle to be built, where he would one day come to himself again, secure, reestablished, reawakening to himself again, slowly, secretly, safely bringing himself out of the sleepwalker's life that had been necessary for his survival.

He waited as his identity returned. It blossomed within him, realms of self and memory fitting themselves into vast empty spaces—but Silverstone stayed with him all the way, showing no sign of fading. He turned to face Gailla and said, "He's still with me . . . I can't get rid of him!"

"He'll keep you company at your trial," Gailla said joylessly.

"But you'll be killing what's left of your old love!" he cried.

"I've been prepared for some time," she said. "They'll wipe you clean and start you up as someone else. It'll be all over for both of us."

"No!" he cried, turned, and rushed to the other door. She did not fire, and he knew that she couldn't, and that he would have enough time to do what he now remembered was his last recourse, waiting for him if something went wrong.

He palmed the door, and still she had not fired. As the door slid open, he knew that she was hesitating, unable to kill the last of her lover. And he felt it also, the mountainous regret at having killed him. He could not banish it, nor the vast cloud of the man's mental remains. It refused to fade away, invading his unused regions with new patterns, and he knew that he was too weak to wipe them out.

The impulse to love had infected him with weak sentiments, and he knew that she felt it also. The bodily memories of their lovemaking had softened them both. That was why she had not killed him as soon as he had regained himself. Or was she preparing him for when she would rebuild her old lover by amplifying the stubborn echoes that remained until they burgeoned and became again the personality she had known? Maybe she knew how to resurrect him and had planned it all along, and would carry out her plan after sufficient revenge had been visited on him.

Well, he would deny her that. He could still take everything from her, and achieve one last victory over a world that had opposed his every desire from the start, always forcing him to take what he wanted. There was nothing else he could do.

"Wait!" she cried as the door opened into chaos. It would have been a way to somewhere, but he had deliberately left it set to no destination—realizing that he might need its sudden exit one day.

As he tumbled into the black obscenity of existence without form, he saw her in the doorway, her mouth open wide in horror and regret, her arms reaching out to him uselessly. And as he felt himself deforming, changing, losing all sense of time and space, he knew that his death would not be quick, that no supernatural damnation could ever have equaled the slow loss of himself that was just beginning.

Gailla was shooting at him now, and he imagined that it was a gesture of pity, an effort to shorten the suffering of what was left of her lover. The third bullet opened his chest, entering slowly, as if unsure of how to obey the laws of physics in this realm. It explored his pain, telling him that he had made this final fate for himself by building the castle and its doorways, with every fleeting, trivial decision—step by inexorable step to one end, to bring him here, to this death.

"Gailla," Silverstone whispered through the pain of her bullet's dancing, failed mercy. "I'm still here."

Then Robles closed his eyes and heard the soft terrible music filtering in from behind the show of things. It was an inhuman music, with nothing of song or dance, or memory in it. It was a music of crushed glass, severed nerves, and brute rumblings, preparing the way for a theme of fear.

And as Robles knew himself in his pain, he yearned for death because Silverstone was still with him.

The Sea of Evening

"Men cannot make angels."
—Darwin

A week had passed since we began to suspect that the Sponge, as we called the Artificial Intelligence Matrix, had gone critical and was achieving self-awareness.

"Have some sympathy," I said as we strolled down the concrete path from the Brain Core Building toward the housing complex. The air was a bit chilly for late summer. A breeze hurried through the maple trees, as if ashamed of being early.

"It is sad about human beings," Ferguson replied as we turned into the setting sun. I shielded my eyes, but Henry looked straight ahead. "They're pressured from within," he said, "by impulses which don't seem to belong to them. Circumstances have rarely permitted much choice, until recent times. You find yourself alive, curious, too often appalled at what is in you and outside you. You balance, but the pincer action wears you down. What's it like for the Sponge, to be born into a black midnight? No sun or stars, only the intricate constellations of insensate knowledge."

The path turned back into the shade, and I took my hand away from my eyes.

"That's very nice," I said, "but I'm far from convinced that it has a localized ego. The Matrix is a simulator, a malleable universe of possibilities." I had admired Henry, looked up to him as a mentor, but his stylish misanthropy had begun to irritate me.

"For now. But elements within an enriched system may achieve individuality and continue developing. Our imaginations are also places where we simulate possibilities, yet we achieve a focused sense of self, however faceted. Even though it is a byproduct of complexity, consciousness plays a vital role. It's a complex feedback loop, contributing to self-control and self-critical guidance. We grew into it from a more automatic state. If you doubt it, look at how we lose ourselves when we're absorbed in something, or dreaming. Self-awareness is as important to higher intelligence as pain."

"That's why bureaucracies are unconscious," I said. "They hate the pain of accurate feedback. Truth upsets the pecking order."

He gave a faint laugh. "Human beings are not yet what they might be."

I shrugged and we walked on in silence. I didn't feel like agreeing with him.

"An android psychologist," he continued suddenly, "might make a human patient feel that he's getting a more objective view of himself. The android brain would of course be lacking the rudimentary brain strata built up during evolutionary survival, so it would be a dispassionate observer in relation to us."

"Well," I said unsurely, "that sounds nice, but it's always been a matter of trying to climb out of our skins and looking back, human or other. You'll only set the regress back one step. We're all locked inside our skulls in the end."

"Objectivity is always relative, never objective, never an unconditional relationship."

I had the feeling that Ferguson was waiting for me to

catch up with some notion of his own.

"What is it, Kevin?" he asked. "Bored?"

I stuck my hands shyly in my pockets and we walked on.

"The Brain Core is likely the first alien on Earth," he said.

I imagined an android John the Baptist striding across the countryside.

"It might begin making doctorly observations about our failings," Ferguson said.

"Not if we raise it right."

"Reminds me of the fear human beings have of their children, that they won't be copies of the previous generation."

"What I meant is that it will be more like us than we realize, if it has to learn from us."

"Perhaps, but it will begin as a relatively free cortex."

I didn't answer.

"Consider your aliens," he went on, as if I had brought up the idea. "Now they might give us a chilling view of humanity."

"Some people have already given us that."

"The Core stands outside evolution's bloody building program. Egoless, free of the ruinous survival impulses emanating from lower mental structures, the Core is an unchained cortex."

No one can see the back of his own neck, and the barber cannot cut his own hair very well. I thought of the faint, hurrying galaxies, and imagined a great circle of civilizations linked in a chain of mutual examination, a vast configuration of observers facing the enigma of space-time, each getting a relative fix on the other.

"Even if alien civilizations exist," I said, "we'll probably never contact one. The universe is too vast, our moments of existence too brief to coincide."

We stopped and I looked at him in the red twilight. His unusually youthful face was blotched with shadows, making his lean shape appear menacing.

"Kevin," he said as he stepped closer and became again the co-researcher I knew, "don't you see?"

"What?"

"You do it all the time, so imagine why we haven't—"

"You can imagine anything."

The chill was getting to my shoulder. I waited in silence.

"Maybe they're waiting before they contact us," he said.

"You mean for us to grow up?"

"Yes, but it's important how."

"Oh, I see. You think the Core will help."

"It's an additional witness to the universe. It can corroborate or discredit our views of things . . . our best foot forward."

"You're hoping for too much," I said.

"I admit that the Core's objectivity will be only relative, but enough for a decent victory over the instinctive, unreflective mind. Better than we've had."

"It's still a long way to controlling wars, modifying politics, or even improving the chanciness of human personal relations." I was feeling contemptuous of him.

"In time," he said, "but consider this. Contact may occur only when other civilizations know that we have escaped the self-torment of our . . . let's say developmental stages. The creation of the Core intelligence might be the proof required."

"What?"

"I know it's ad hoc from your point of view. . . ."

I took a deep breath. "It's laughable, Henry! You assume a damned versus the elect theology. Only those who attain a virtuous state will be contacted from the skies."

He took out his already packed pipe and lighter in one motion, lit the tobacco and puffed up an angry cloud; for a moment the flame made his face seem grotesque. It was all over for him, I thought.

"How would they even know?" I asked, humoring him.

"They would keep informed."

"Pretty religious of you. Credits and demerits all go into a big book up there."

"Damn, this thing's gone out."

I looked up at the sky, newly swept clean by the unseasonably cold air pushing in from the north. If Henry had a breakdown, I would be promoted.

"You were always fairly orthodox, Kevin, even in your personal life. Never do anything if it means a risk or sacrifice."

"Fairly's the right word," I answered. "Why endanger past work without reasonable evidence?"

"Play the game until it fails." He relit his pipe with the dancing flame.

"Come on, Henry. You're abasing yourself before hypothetical superiors. Fine and good for speculations, but I'd hate to see this creeping into your work."

"Don't you look up to anyone? We search for fathers or sons among those we befriend . . . bits and pieces of what should have been fathers, or may have been sons, daughters . . ." He seemed very nervous about his pipe.

"Come on," I said finally, feeling a bit embarrassed by his question. "They would have to have observers to know." A horde of objections clamored for my attention.

"What if you can't see your game is failing?"

"Then you're swept away. It's a risk you have to take."

"Ah, there," he said, puffing his bowl into a glow.

It had grown dark, and we had not gone even halfway to the housing complex. I looked back to the now brightly lit dome of the Brain Core Building, where something newly aware was reaching out of its private darkness. A week now.

Stars appeared, brightening as twilight faded. Ferguson had made me feel the great outwardness; but the inner regions waited everywhere, vast and cavernous, inhabited by uncontrollable, fear-filled beasts, cruel and raging. Madness resonates in those realms, crying with a brassy music. Even if we could travel to the suns of Orion, anywhere in the big black, the inner abyss would go with us. Could it be closed off? Should it be closed off? How many intelligent species had asked this question, made the effort, and failed?

Henry's wristphone beeped.

"Yes?"

"Are you alone?" a small voice asked.

"I'm with Doctor Flew."

"Security is ordering everyone indoors at once. Return to the Core Building."

"Yes, of course," Henry said, puffing with ease.

"Well, it's been intriguing," I said, raising my voice above the whisper of the wind in the trees. "Clever to think that we would be contacted as we transcend our old brains through the birth of artificial intelligences. But how can I buy it? Saviors from the stars, arriving to pat us on the head for having awakened our better self? It's a bit vague, you have to admit."

"Well, they wouldn't come just to reveal their presence, but . . . to deposit information in our developing Core, as a gift for the future. It would all be very discreet, I would imagine, nothing to cause culture shock."

I stared at his dark shape.

"Then, of course," he continued dryly, "the Brain Core

would become an avenue of communication, a reliable intermediary between the species. The problem of communicating with actual alien individuals would be bypassed, thus avoiding embarrassing misunderstandings. Frequent contact between individuals would come later."

I suddenly knew what he would claim next.

"Yes, I'm with them," he said. "Humans have been taken from here routinely: raised, educated, and returned."

"Guardian angels . . ." I muttered. Henry had lost his mind. His phone began to beep, but he ignored it. He turned and his face caught the light from the Core Building. He gazed at me directly, in a way I had not known, without guile, it seemed; for the first time in my life I felt that I was looking into the mind of a genuinely free intelligence. He made me feel that I was the slow wit, the last to catch on that the darkness of human history was ending. I suppose most madmen have this capacity for imposing a vision. My future was assured, I realized.

"Henry," I said patiently, for friendship's sake. "It's not true. Don't you see, how can it—"

"Open your eyes," he said as my phone added its beep to his. My shoulder ached and the chill wind whispered painfully in my ears as I looked up.

Lights which were not stars began to appear in the sea of evening.

Henry's pipe clattered on the walkway, as if he had discarded it. He stood motionless.

"I hope to hell you know what you're doing," I said as the lights drew nearer.

The Middle Distance

Heathen God

". . . every heathen deity has its place in the flow of existence."

The isolation station and preserve for alien flora and fauna on Antares IV had only one prisoner, a three-foot-tall gnome-like biped with skin like creased leather and eyes like great glass globes. His hair was silky white and reached down to his shoulders, and he usually went about the great natural park naked. He lived in a small white cell located in one of the huge block-like administration modules. There was a small bed in the cell, and a small doorway which led out of the park. A hundred feet away from the door there was a small pool, one of many scattered throughout the park. It reflected the deep-blue color of the sky.

The gnome was very old, but no one had yet determined quite how old. And there seemed to be no way to find out. The gnome himself had never volunteered any information about his past. In the one hundred years of his imprisonment he had never asked the caretaker for anything. It was rumored among the small staff of Earthmen and humanoids that the gnome was mad. Generally they avoided him. Sometimes they would watch his small figure gazing at the giant disk of Antares hanging blood red on the horizon, just above the well-pruned trees of the park, and they would wonder what he might be thinking.

The majority of Earthpeoples spread over twelve star systems did not even know of the gnome's existence, much less his importance. A few knew, but they were mostly scholarly and political figures, and a few theologians. The most important fact about the alien was that sometime in the remote past he had been responsible for the construction of the solar system and the emergence of intelligent life on Earth.

The secret had been well kept for over a century.

In the one hundred and fourth year of the alien's captivity, two men set out to visit him. The first man's motives were practical: the toppling of an old regime; the other man's goal was to ask questions. The first man's political enemies had helped him to undertake this journey, seeing that it would give them the chance to destroy him. The importance of gaining definitive information about the alien was in itself enough reason to send a mission, but combined with what they knew about the motives of the man they feared, this mission would provide the occasion to resolve both matters at the same time. The second man would bring back anything of value that they might learn about the gnome.

Everything had been planned down to the last detail. The first ship, carrying the two unsuspecting men, was almost ready to come out of hyperspace near Antares. Two hours behind it in the warp was a military vessel—a small troop ship. As the first vessel came out of nothingness into the brilliance of the great star, the commander of the small force ship opened his sealed orders.

As he came down the shuttle ramp with his two companions, Father Louis Chavez tried to prepare himself for what he would find here. It was still difficult to believe what his superiors had told him about the imprisoned alien. The morning air of Antares IV was fresh, and the immediate impression was one of stepping out into a warm botanical garden. At his left Sister Guinivere carried his small attaché case. On his right walked Benedict Compton, linguist, cultural anthropologist and as everyone took for granted, eventual candidate for first secretary of Earth's Northern Hemisphere. Compton was potentially a religious man, but the kind who always demanded an advance guarantee before committing himself to anything. Chavez felt suspicious of him.

On Earth the religio-philosophic system was a blend of evolutionary Chardinism and Christianity, an imposing intellectual structure that had been dominant for some two hundred years now. The political structure based its legitimacy and continuing policies on it. Compton, from what he had learned, had frightened some high authorities with the claim that the gnome creature here on Antares IV was a potential threat to the beliefs of mankind. This, combined with what was already known about the alien's past, was seemingly enough to send this fact-finding mission. Only a few men knew about it, and Chavez remembered the fear he had sensed in them when he had been briefed. Their greatest fear was that somehow the gnome's history would become public knowledge. Compton, despite his motives, had found a few more political friends. But Chavez suspected that Compton wanted power not for himself, but to do something about the quality of life on Earth. He was sure the man was sincere. How little of the thought in our official faith filters out into actual policy, Chavez thought. And what would the government do if an unorganized faith—a heresy in the old sense — were to result from this meeting between Compton and the alien? Then he remembered how Compton had rushed this whole visit. He wondered just how far a man like Compton would go to have his way in the world.

Antares was huge on the horizon, a massive red disk against a deep blue sky. A slight breeze waved the trees around the landing square. The pathway, which started at the north corner, led to three bright white buildings set on a neat lawn and surrounded by flowering shrubs and fruit-bearing trees. The walk was pleasant.

Rufus Kade, the caretaker, met them at the front entrance to the main building. He showed them into the comfortable reception room. He was a tall, thin botanist, who had taken the post because it gave him the opportunity to be near exotic plants. Some of the flora came from worlds as much as one hundred light-years away from Antares. After the introductions were over, Kade took the party to the garden where the gnome spent most of his time.

"Do you ever talk with him, Mr. Kade?" Father Chavez asked. The caretaker shook his head. "No," he said. "And now I hope you will excuse me, I have work to do." He left them at the entrance to the garden path.

Compton turned to Father Chavez and said, "You are lucky, you're the only representative of any church ever to get a chance to meet what might be the central deity of that church." He smiled. "But I feel sorry for you—for whatever he is, he will not be what you expect, and most certainly he will not be what you want him to be."

"Let's wait and see," Chavez said. "I'm not a credulous man."

"You know, Chavez," Compton said in a more serious mood, "they let me come here too easily. What I mean is they took my word for the danger involved with little or no question."

"Should they have not taken your word? You are an important man."

Sister Guinivere led the way into the garden. On either side of them the plants were luxurious, with huge green leaves and strange varicolored flowers. The air was filled with rich scents, and the Earth gave the sensation of being very moist and loosely packed. They came into the open area surrounding the pool. Sister Guinivere stood between the two men as they looked at the scene. The water was still, and the disk of Antares was high enough now in the morning sky to be reflected in it.

The gnome stood on the far side, watching them as they approached, as if he expected them at any moment to break into some words of greeting. It would be awkward standing before a member of a race a million years older than mankind and towering over him. It would be aesthetically banal, Chavez thought.

As they came to the other side of the pool Compton said, "Let me start the conversation, Father."

"If you wish," Chavez said. *Why am I afraid, and what does it matter who starts the conversation,* he thought.

Compton walked up to the gnome and sat down cross-legged in front of him. It was a diplomatic gesture. Father Chavez felt relieved and followed the example, motioning Sister Guinivere to do the same. They all looked at the small alien.

His eyes were deep-set and large; his hair was white, thin and reached down to his shoulders. He had held his hand behind his back when they had approached, but now they were together in front of him. His shoulders were narrow and his arms were thin. He wore a one-piece coverall with short sleeves.

Chavez hoped they would be able to talk to him easily. The gnome looked at each of them in turn. It became obvious that he expected them to start the conversation.

"My name is Benedict Compton," Compton said, "and this is Father Chavez and Sister Guinivere, his secretary. We came here to ask you about your past, because it concerns us."

Slowly the gnome nodded his head, but he did not sit with them. Compton gave Chavez a questioning look.

"Could you tell us who you are?" Chavez asked. The gnome moved his head sharply to look at him. *It's almost as if I interrupted him at something,* Chavez thought. There was a sad look on the face now, as if in that one moment he had understood everything—why they were here and the part he would have to play.

Chavez felt his stomach grow tense. He felt as if he were being carefully examined. Compton was playing with a blade of grass. Sister Guinivere sat with her hands folded in her lap. Briefly he recalled the facts he knew about the alien—facts which only a few Earthmen had been given access to over the last century. Facts which demanded that some sort of official attitude be taken.

The best-kept secret of the past century was the fact that this small creature had initiated the events which led to the emergence of intelligent life on Earth. In the far past he had harnessed his powers of imagination to a vast machine, which had been built for another purpose, and had used it to create much of the life on Earth. He had been caught at his experiments and exiled. Long before men had gone out to the stars he had been a wanderer in the galaxy, but in recent years he had been handed over to Earth authorities to keep at this extraterrestrial preserve. Apparently his people still feared his madness. This was all they had ever revealed to the few Earthmen who took charge of the matter.

It was conjectured that the gnome's race was highly isolationist; the gnome was the only member of it who had ever been seen by Earthmen. The opinion was that his culture feared contact with other intelligent life, and especially with this illegitimate creation. Of the few who knew about the case, one or two had expressed disbelief. It was after all, Chavez thought, enough to make any man uneasy. It seemed safer to ignore the matter most of the time.

Since that one contact with Earth, the gnome's race had never come back for him. A century ago they had simply left him in Earth orbit, in a small vessel of undeniably superior workmanship. A recorded message gave all the information they had wanted to reveal. Their home world had never been found, and the gnome had remained silent. Benedict Compton had set up this meeting, and Chavez had been briefed by his superiors and instructed to go along as an observer.

Chavez remembered how the information had at first shaken and then puzzled him. The tension in his stomach grew worse. He wondered about Compton's motives, but he had not dared to question them openly. On Earth many scientists prized the alien as the only contact with a truly advanced culture, and he knew that more than one young student would do anything to unlock the secrets that must surely exist in the brain of the small being now standing in front of him. He felt sure that Compton was hoping for some such thing.

Suddenly the small figure took a step back from them. A small breeze waved his long white hair. His small, gnarly body took on a strange stature; his face was grief-stricken and his low voice was sad. It wavered as he spoke to them. "I made you to love each other, and through yourselves, me. I needed that love. No one can know how much I needed it, but it had to be freely given, so I had to permit the possibility of it being withheld. There was no other way, and there still is not."

Chavez looked at Compton. The big man sat very still. Sister Guinivere was looking down at the grass in front of her feet. Chavez felt a stirring of fear and panic in his insides. It felt as if the alien was speaking only to him—as if *he* could relieve the thirst that lived behind those deep-set eyes in that small head.

He felt the other's need. He felt the deprivation that was visible on that face, and he felt that at any moment he would feel the awesome rage that would spill out onto them. This then, he thought, is the madness that his race had spoken about. All the power had been stripped from this being, and now he was a beggar.

Instead of rage there was sadness. It was oppressive. What was Compton trying to uncover here? How could all this benefit anyone? Chavez felt his left hand shaking, and he gripped it with the other hand.

The gnome raised his right hand and spoke again. *Dear God, help me,* Chavez prayed. *Help me to see this clearly.* "I fled from the hive mind which my race was working toward," the gnome said in a louder voice than before. "They have achieved it. They are one entity now. What you see in this dwarfed body are only the essentials of myself—the feelings mostly—they wait for the day when the love in my children comes to fruition and they will unite, thus recreating my former self—which is now in them. Then I will leave my prison and return to them to become the completion of myself. This body will die then. My longing for that time is without limit, and I will make another history like this one and see it through. Each time I will be the completion of a species and its moving spirit. And again they will give birth to me. Without this I am nothing."

There was a loud thunderclap overhead, the unmistakable sound of a shuttle coming through the atmosphere. *But it was too early for the starship shuttle to be coming back for them,* Chavez thought. Compton jumped up and turned to look toward the administration buildings. Chavez noticed that the gnome was looking at him. *Do your people worship a supreme being?* Chavez thought the question. *Do they have the idea of such a being? Surely you know the meaning of such a being?*

I don't know any such thing. The thought was clear in his head. *Do you know him?*

"It's a shuttle craft," Compton said.

Chavez got up. Sister Guinivere struggled to her feet. "What is it?" she asked.

"I—I don't know who it could be," Compton said. Chavez noticed the lack of confidence in the other's voice. Behind them the gnome stood perfectly still, unaffected by the interruption.

"They've landed by now," Compton said. "It could only be one thing, Father—they've found out my plans for the gnome." Compton spoke in a low voice. "Father, this is the only way to get a change on Earth—yes, it's what you think, a cult, with me as its head, but the cause is just. Join me now, Father!"

Then it's true, Chavez thought. *He's planning to by-pass the lawful candidacy. Then why did they let him come here?*

There was a rustling in the shrubs around the pool area. Suddenly they were surrounded by armed men. Twenty figures in full battle gear had stepped out from the trees and garden shrubs. They stood perfectly still, waiting.

Antares was directly overhead now, a dark-red circle of light covering ten percent of the blue dome that was the sky. Noontime.

Compton's voice shook as he shouted, "What is *this?* Who the devil are you!"

A tall man immediately on the other side of the pool from them appeared to be the commanding officer. He wore no gear and there were no weapons in his hands. Instead he held a small piece of paper which he had just taken out of a sealed envelope.

"Stand away, Father, and you too, Sister!" the officer shouted. "This does not concern you." Then he looked down at the paper in his hand and read: "Benedict Compton, you have been charged with conspiracy to overthrow the government of the Northern Hemisphere on Earth by unlawful means, and you have been tried and convicted by the high court of North America for this crime. The crime involves the use of an alien being as your co-conspirator to initiate a religious controversy through a personally financed campaign which would result in your becoming the leader of a subversive cult, whose aim would be to seize power through a carefully prepared hoax. You and your co-conspirator are both mortal enemies of the state." The officer folded the paper and put it back in its envelope and placed it in his tunic.

Chavez noticed that Sister Guinivere was at his side, and he could tell that she was afraid.

Compton turned to Chavez. "Father, protect the gnome, whatever he is. Use what authority you have. They won't touch you."

"The execution order is signed by Secretary Alcibiad herself!" the tall officer shouted.

Chavez was silent.

"Father, please!" Compton pleaded. "You can't let this happen." Chavez heard the words, but he was numb with surprise. The words had transfixed him as effectively as any spear. He couldn't move, he couldn't think. Sister Guinivere held his arm.

Suddenly Compton was moving toward the gnome.

"Shoot!"

The lasers reached out like tongues.

The little figure fell. And the thought went out from him in one last effort, reaching light-years into space. *I loved you. You did not love me, or each other.* They all heard the thought, and it stopped them momentarily. Compton was still standing, but his right arm was gone, and he was bleeding noisily onto the grass.

"Shoot!"

Again the lasers lashed out. Compton fell on his back, a few yards from the gnome. Sister Guinivere collapsed to her knees, sobbing. She began to wail. The soldiers began to retreat. Father Chavez sat down on the ground. He didn't know what to do. He looked at the two bodies. There was smoke coming from Compton's clothing. The gnome's hair was aflame.

The tall officer now stood alone on the other side of the pool. Chavez knew that his orders had probably been sealed, and he only now felt their full force. After a few moments the tall officer turned and went after his men.

The alien knew this would happen, Chavez thought. *He knew, and that was why he told us everything.*

When the great disk of Antares was forty-five degrees above the horizon, Rufus Kade came out to them. He put the two bodies in plastic specimen bags. Sister Guinivere was calm now and was holding Father Chavez's hand. They both stood up when Kade finished with the bodies.

"They had an official pass from way up," Kade said. "I even checked back on it."

He walked slowly with them to the administration building.

Father Chavez sat alone in his small cabin looking at the small monitor which showed him where he had been. Soon now the brilliance of the stars would be replaced by the dull emptiness of hyperspace. Antares was a small red disk on the screen.

Momentarily Chavez resented the fact that he had been a mere creation to the gnome. In any case the alien had not been God. His future importance would be no greater than that of Christ—probably less. He had been only an architect, a mere shaper of materials which had existed long before even his great race had come into being. But still—was he not closer to God than any *man* had ever been? Or would be?

The completion for which the gnome had made man would never take place now. The point of mankind's existence as he had made it was gone. And the alien had not known God. If there was such a being, a greatest possible being, he now seemed hopelessly remote . . .

O Lord, I pray for a sign! Chavez thought.

But he heard only his thoughts and nothing from the being who would surely have answered in a case like this. And he had stood by while they killed the gnome there in the garden by the pool, on that planet circling the red star whose diameter was greater than the orbit of Mars. Despite all his reasoning now, Chavez knew that he had stood back while they killed that part of the small creature which had loved humanity.

But what had he said? The *rest* of the gnome's being *was* humanity, and it still existed; except that now it would never be reunited with him. "Do not fear," the holy Antony had said three thousand years ago, "this goodness as a thing impossible, nor its pursuit as something alien, set a great way off: it hangeth on our own arbitrament. For the sake of the Greek learning men go overseas . . . but the city of God is everywhere . . . the kingdom of God is within. The goodness that is in us only asks the human mind." *What we can do for ourselves,* Chavez thought, *that's all that is ours now.*

He took a deep breath as the starship slipped into the nothingness of hyperspace. He felt the burden of the political power which he now carried as a witness to the alien's murder, and he knew that Compton's life had not been for nothing. He would have to hide his intentions carefully, but he knew what he would have to do.

In time, he hoped anew, we may still give birth to the semblance of godhood that lives on in mankind, on that small world which circles a yellow sun.

Wayside World

The city sat in the hill, rising upward from deep within the mass of Earth, rock and vegetation to tower a kilometer into the night sky, its angled windows dark, reflecting only the bright stars and the faint rainbow of the ring; ten thousand windows, centuries old and unbroken, staring westward across the valley. Meteors flashed in the plastic panes, mute fireworks showing in black, sightless eyes long past celebration. The structure was an empty shell which had once housed a million people. A few still used it because the windows caught the sunlight, warming the outer layer of dwelling spaces through trapped heat.

At the edge of the world a morning storm flickered in the clouds which hid the dawnlight. The city's clear panels became blinking eyes, the sudden brightness of lightning destroying the mirrored ebony surfaces which held the cold starlight and dying meteor trails.

I

In rooms a third of the way up from the vegetation of the hill-side, six people slept, derelicts in need of a dawn to stir them from their troubled sleep . . .

He opened his eyes suddenly and saw the light flashing through the windows, flooding the world with a blue-white wash. In a moment the drops were beating against the win-dows, running like tears down the inclines. The rain would make things grow; summer would last just a little longer.

Sadness welled up within him. He started to repeat his name in the way his mother had once spoken it.

Call him Ishbok, his father had said a long time ago, but his mother had made it sound special. *Ishbok,* he whispered softly to himself, trying to catch the musical quality of his mother's voice.

The others did not waken, and the storm seemed to rage over their stillness. The water washed downward in a river; the thunder walked with the footsteps of a giant. The full force of the storm rode over the valley, holding back the light of sunrise.

Ishbok looked around at his sleeping companions, at Foler, who also wanted Anneka; at Foler's younger brother, Thessan, who would never be well; at Anneka sleeping next to her dying parents. The old couple were fading fast, sleeping away most of each day; there was nothing to be done except make them comfortable and bring them what little food they were able to eat. *Why could we not have been trees,* Ishbok thought, *or the stones which seem able to keep their pride. We are so soft and filled with blood, and a dried sarissa bamboo point is enough to kill us. . . .*

Foler already spoke as if Anneka belonged to him. His every glance was a challenge. Ishbok was avoiding a fight, hoping that Anneka would say how she felt. Sometimes he felt shamed and angry at her silence. He did not want to fight Foler, even if a fair fight were possible; Thessan would join in like a stupid dog defending his master. The dark-haired older brother's friendly smile hid the truth—he was always ready to let things happen, as long as they served his wants.

After Anneka's mother and father died, Foler would take the daughter. If Ishbok tried to stop it, he would die; if he did nothing, he would live. It was as simple as that. *He's afraid to take her while the old live,* Ishbok thought. *He's afraid of their curses. He fears unseen things more than me. He controls Thessan with his own fears. . . .*

For a moment Ishbok imagined what it would be like to be Thessan. Without Foler, nothing was certain. Foler knew where all the food was to be hunted or found; he kept evil things away at night. Foler had to be obeyed; there was no other way. Foler made him feel good; Foler made him feel safe.

Thessan was like a faber, except fabers were much more alert; fabers had pride. Ishbok felt sorry for Thessan; but being sorry would not help him, as hatred would not make his brother better.

Across the room Foler stirred and sat up while prodding Thessan awake. His eyes were watchful, suspicious; but in a moment his gaze became uncaring as he realized that Ishbok would not have waited for wakefulness to kill him. Slowly Foler got to his feet. *He knows I couldn't do it, he's sure of it.*

"Coward!" Foler threw the word like a stone.

Anneka woke up, pulling the blanket around her for protection. She sat up and looked at Ishbok. He thought he saw reproach in her expression, but the light was too faint to be sure. There would be no smile or look of sympathy, only the look of resignation. *Anneka . . . Anneka,* he said silently, *I made none of this, but I love you.*

"Unwind your stringy muscles," Foler said to him, "we have food to find."

The thunder exploded again and water ran in noisy rivulets on the windows. Foler's face was a grinning skull with caves for eyes.

Anneka began to braid her long brown hair, her eyes cast downward. She looked up only to glance at the storm outside.

Ishbok watched her from where he sat on his blanket. His stomach was cold and empty. He shivered, longing for the warm sun and hoping the storm would pass soon; it would make food searching a little easier . . .

Anneka's father woke up, breathing badly and coughing.

"The old fool should be dead," Foler said, stretching. Then he held out a hand and helped Thessan stand up.

Anneka's mother woke up, wailing about her blindness.

"Keep her quiet," Foler said. Ishbok saw a fearful look take hold of Foler's face. "They should both be dead."

"They'll die, they'll die," Thessan chanted, hoping to please his brother. Foler grinned and patted him on the back.

Suddenly Thessan lumbered across the large room to a window and placed his large palms against the moisture-laden interior surface. He washed his face, chuckling to himself.

"It's a dark rainy morning," Anneka said to her mother, stroking her forehead. Her husband reached over and held her bony hand. The old woman cleared her throat.

Foler went over to the window and slapped some moisture on his face. Ishbok stumbled to his feet and walked over to a fresh window. He cupped some wetness and put it to his face.

Foler laughed. "Not much hair to wash on him."

Ishbok looked up to see Thessan standing next to him, grinning and running his fingers through his dirty beard.

Ishbok turned away from him and took a few steps toward the door.

Anneka tied her braids off with two bits of leather and stood up. "I'm ready," she said.

Foler went past Ishbok and turned around in the door. "A strong woman—not for you. With that soft hide of yours, you'd bleed to death from her scratches."

Ishbok felt the anger swell in himself, but he looked away from Foler's eyes.

"You're not worth killing," Foler continued. "One day you'll break your own neck and save me the trouble. You're good for picking roots, berries and nuts. Even Anneka can kill an animal for food." He paused. "Ah, let's get going!" He turned and went out into the hall and toward the stairs. Ishbok followed, thinking suddenly that he might run up behind Foler and push him to his death; but in the next moment he was flat on his face as Thessan pulled his feet out from behind. Ishbok's jaw hurt from the impact. Thessan stumbled across him and ran after his brother, laughing.

Anneka helped him to his feet and walked toward the stairs without a word. Slowly Ishbok followed, feeling no hatred now, only shame and sadness, the coldness in his stomach a heavy weight slowing his steps.

Foler led them upstream through the center of the valley. Thessan followed close behind him. Anneka walked a dozen paces behind Thessan. Ishbok was last.

The clouds of morning passed. Anneka's hair turned a bright red in the sun rising at their back. Ishbok walked slowly, watching her. Despite her clothing from the oldtime, the patched trousers, leather belt, sweater and boots, she seemed gentle marching across the mossy turf next to the stream.

Morning mists rose from the valley as the sun warmed the Earth. The silence of his own breathing and the steadiness of the stream at his right calmed him. Far ahead to his left the red-coned evergreens sat on the mountainside; around them nestled sugarroot bushes, their leaves and pulpy twigs laden with the sweetness of late summer.

Slowly Foler was making a circle which would lead them

up into the hills. They would eat the sugarroot, and then there would be enough strength to bring down some game and carry it home. Ishbok licked his lips at the thought of the sugarroot.

Maybe today they would bring down a hipposaur when it came to drink the stream water and graze on the green moss; maybe today luck would give them enough food for a week's rest in the city.

But quickly he remembered that full stomachs and rested muscles would help them forget the need they all had of one another. Foler would want Anneka again; Thessan would be bored and hard to control.

A jumpingtom raced across Foler's path. Foler raised his boomerang and let fly, cursing as it missed. He went to get it back. Ishbok heard more cursing.

"Ishbok, come here!" Foler shouted.

Ishbok hurried.

"It broke on the stone—you'll have to make a new one. Better make two."

Foler was almost friendly.

If I make too many spares, Ishbok thought, *you won't need me.* "I can only work so fast," he said softly, "and not at all when I'm hungry and afraid."

Foler's dark eyes were scornful. His eyebrows went up and he grinned through his beard. "I'm the best thrower."

Foler turned away and continued on the path to the sugarroots. Ishbok followed. Thessan came up behind him and pushed him out of the way to get back near his brother. Ishbok turned his head to see Anneka walking steadily behind him. She did not look up and he turned away to fix his gaze on the red cones ahead.

As he walked he thought of the stories about the old sicknesses, the war plagues, the fireballs that left heaps of dead, the skeletons in the cities. He had never seen any of these things, but his mother's vivid tellings lived in his mind. He remembered his father's look of reproach when he would find her giving such life to the past.

Those who lived had found each other among the dead, in cities which stood unharmed, yet were gutted. The survivors knew the value of human life, acting out of necessity, clinging to each other in resignation and acceptance. So it had been for more than two generations. Ishbok's father and mother had met in the great empty city by the northern lake. From there they had travelled down to the southern ocean, in time for Ishbok to be born in a small stone house near the water. His father had complained that there were few old-time libraries in the smaller southern cities, and that Ishbok would not survive as well in a colder climate.

But life will be easier here, his mother had said, *and we don't have to go back.*

He'll have to go back to learn, his father had answered.

When he is older, he'll go back well enough . . .

One day dark men had come out of the swamp to spear his father to a gnarly dwarf tree and carry his mother away like a four-footed animal hanging from a stick, her long black hair dragging on the ground . . .

Ishbok remembered the sick feeling in his stomach as he had been picked up and hurled down from a cliff into the sea. But his small body had missed the rocks. His cheek touched bottom gently and he pushed himself upward with his hands. He swam as he had been taught and the waves washed him ashore with only a few cuts from the rocks. He remembered his own blood on the sand when he had gotten up hours later, his tears burned away by the hot sun.

The little house was empty when he returned. In the silence of sea and memory he heard again his father's wish that he should learn about the world before life came to an end. When he looked at the body pinned to the tree, he imagined that his father's life had become joined to the twisted trunk, his flesh drinking now the moisture brought up by the tree's deeply searching roots.

Traveling north, he had searched for the libraries which held the books he knew how to read. He could not read all the languages brought to his world, Cleopatra, by the colonists from Earth, but he could always understand his own, and much of two others. The libraries spoke about one another, sending him amongst themselves as would jealous guardians who share a favorite child. The old buildings gave him shelter and knowledge—the knowledge of stored foods and where to find them. In winter the food enabled him to stay in one place as he studied. Once he had been forced to burn a few of the books he could not read to keep warm, telling himself that he would never find anyone who could tell him what they were about. Besides, the books spoke of other kinds of books, known things stored in machines which gave knowledge for the asking; he was sure there was more than one copy of the volumes he had burned.

In the empty cities he had come upon small bands of men and women. Sometimes they would accept him, with suspicion; he would stay for a time, to leave or to be driven off sooner or later.

He had come into Anneka's group five summers ago. Her parents could still walk then. Foler and Thessan had been friendly, especially after finding out he could make knives, spear points and boomerangs—and keep the weapons sharper than they had ever known. But no matter how long Foler watched him work the old metal on the stream stones, he could not match Ishbok's skill. One day Thessan had tried sharpening to please his brother. Foler had beaten him for ruining two knives, but Ishbok had saved the edges.

So little of what he had learned in the libraries could be turned into useful things. Knowledge had made him feel pity, and the need for another kind of learning, barely glimpsed, one which might again create the realities of the old time.

Ishbok turned to look back at the city, set like a blue gem in the mossy mountain, entranceways hidden in foliage. The towering place was always a reminder of exile from a better past. The structure soared upward, a relic of powers he could not summon; the sight gave him hope, at the same time making him feel small. He felt anger in his humiliation, and turned quickly to follow Foler and Thessan before Anneka caught up to him.

Foler and Thessan were on their knees eating leaves from the sugarroot bushes. Ishbok sat down under a red-coned evergreen and picked a leaf from the nearest bush. Anneka was only a few paces behind him. She came up past him and sat down near the brothers without looking at him.

Ishbok swallowed the sweet juice and spit out the pulp. His stomach rumbled.

"Fabers!" Foler whispered loudly.

They all stood up and turned to look where he was pointing. On the angle of the mountainside, shapes stood among the evergreens, scaly manlike forms with long necks and slender tails.

Receding clouds let sunlight fall between the trees, scattering patches of bluish yellow on mossy rocks and soft Earth. Somewhere a tree spook cried out and was still, reminding Ishbok of the colorfully plumed jack-dandies he had known as a child. In the silence of sun and shadow, the fabers began to move, stepping softly, surely, as if the evergreens had sprouted legs.

As the saurians moved in and out of sunlight, Ishbok saw the v-shaped mouths of the closest ones, set in the familiar grin; the golden eyes were wide under ridges, the skullcap crests suggesting the helmets of old time warriors from other times, other worlds.

But these fabers would not fight; they moved too slowly. These were not like the changed ones who had once fought for men. These were the dying ones, easy to kill and eat, yet they seemed to mock their destroyers.

Foler loosed his remaining good boomerang. It flew between the trees like a diving cinnamon bat and felled the forward faber. The creature tumbled down the incline while its companions stopped and switched their tails in agitation.

"Better than pig," Thessan said as he stopped the body's roll with his foot.

"We can cut it up and go home," Foler said.

Ishbok watched the single slit nostril of the dying faber as it drew in air in hungry rasps. The mouth was open, revealing the nearly human teeth set in a delicate jaw.

Thessan picked up a large rock and caved in the skull. When he stepped back the golden eyes were closed. The claw-tipped hands unclenched.

Ishbok looked up the mountainside, but the rest of the fabers were gone, leaving a mournful silence for the one who had died.

"Lucky it was not a killer pack," Foler said. He knelt down with Anneka and his brother. Together they began to cut up the body with their knives, selecting the best portions.

"We'll cut some hide to carry the meat in," Foler said.

Ishbok's stomach rumbled again, loudly enough to be heard. Foler laughed at the sound and continued cutting.

My knives, Ishbok thought. For Anneka the flesh meant a few days of life for her parents, and a more comfortable dying. Ishbok turned away as Thessan started to chew a piece of uncooked flesh.

"Here," Foler said. Ishbok turned to receive a wrapped cut of meat. "You carry one if you want to eat." *For Anneka's sake,* he told himself. "One day we'll find their eggs," Foler added.

A wind came up as the sun neared noon. It rushed through the trees like an angry thing. Red cones fell as if they were solid drops of blood. Ishbok thought that at any moment the wind would cry out in a shriek above its own fearful whispering.

As they marched back toward the city, Ishbok knew that he would eat the faber's meat with the others. His portion was not very heavy, but they were all weak from the morning's march; the meat held them together with its promise of rest. He would eat the meat as long as it was cooked, however badly.

Across the valley the city was a mirrored sheet of golden sunlight set against the hills, rising upward to a spear point in a blue sky. Ishbok wondered as he walked behind Foler and Thessan and Anneka. He tried to imagine all the things that he would never know—the skills which enabled men to live longer, heal their wounds, reach beyond the world.

He remembered reading about the giant city which sat on Charmian, Moon-sister of the world; beings like himself had made a place for themselves there also. Others had travelled through the space between worlds, perhaps even to other stars.

Behind the city's spear point there was a large flat place where flying machines had once come to land, leaving off travellers and picking up new ones. He had seen a picture in a book. Long ago he had promised himself that he would climb up there, if he ever found the city. From that place, he had imagined, he would see more than anyone had seen in a long time.

Ishbok lay on his blankets in the corner of the room. Thessan was urinating on the small fire near the open window. The smell of burnt meat was still strong, despite the cool evening air drafting from the window through the door into the corridor. Anneka was with her parents, speaking softly to them. Foler lay on his blankets in the corner opposite from Ishbok. Anneka's parents had not been able to eat much. Half of the carcass was still uncooked.

"Fire's out," Thessan said.

The shadows of sunset seemed almost purple; the windows were panels of airy blue. Ishbok closed his eyes and saw the faber's face in the moment before the wise golden eyes had closed.

"Fire's out," Thessan repeated.

"Go to sleep," Foler said.

In time, Ishbok told himself, Anneka would belong completely to Foler and his brother. He saw himself moving on to another place, another group. If Anneka became heavy with Foler's child, that would be enough. Foler would lose an edge-maker: Ishbok would lose Anneka. *I have no courage,* he said to himself.

Ishbok opened his eyes and saw stars twinkling brightly in a darkening sky. His eyes were heavy. He felt uncaring in the tired satisfaction of his full stomach. Thessan had gone to lie down next to his brother. They were sleeping beasts and could not harm him. Faber faces mocked him when his eyes closed; yet their expressions also seemed pitying. A dark tide came in upon him, billowing clouds of darkness carrying him away from all awareness.

II

Anneka's sobbing woke him near dawn. He lifted his head and saw her kneeling over her parents, a dark form against the pale light coming in through the windows.

He raised himself and crawled toward her, until he could see the old couple lying together in death. He got up on his knees and was still. Anneka did not look at him as she hovered over the lumpy masses of the dead.

Thessan began to snore loudly.

Ishbok knew that the old ones could not have lived much longer. Both had been more than thirty years old, though he had read that in the old time people had lived to a hundred. Even so the feeling of uselessness had contributed to their death.

In the corner beyond, Foler woke up to watch. Thessan began to snore even more loudly than before. Foler poked him in the ribs and the snoring stopped.

Anneka lay down next to her parents as if to imitate their stillness. In his corner Foler lay back and went to sleep. Ishbok moved backward on his knees and crawled under his blankets.

After a while sleep returned. Gratefully, he drifted away from the presence of death.

He awoke after what seemed a very long time, but the

pale light of dawn was not much brighter than before. He sat up and looked around the room. Anneka was not with her parents. He peered across the room and saw her bare shoulders next to Foler's.

Ishbok got up on all fours and started to crawl toward her, his heart a cold stone in his chest. In a moment he saw that her dark eyes were open wide, staring at the ceiling as she clutched her portion of the gray blanket.

A whistle of air escaped from Thessan, who now slept a dozen paces away, like a dog who had been driven away for the night.

Ishbok stopped crawling. Anneka turned her head and looked at him, staring at him as if from out of a dark cave.

"Get away!" she whispered, baring her teeth grotesquely.

"Anneka . . ."

Foler awoke suddenly, saw him, and laughed. "Swine," Ishbok said softly.

Foler propped himself up on one elbow and regarded him with mock seriousness. "If you weren't so useful I would kill you. Maybe I'd let Thessan do it."

"Go away," Anneka said. "Don't fight with him."

Ishbok stood up and said, "I'm leaving this morning."

Foler looked uncertain as he stood up wearing only his pants and boots.

Ishbok felt all his muscles tense as the thought of having been wrong about Anneka took hold of him. What did she see in Foler, who would lend her to his brother as easily as he would spit. He looked into her eyes, but they still stared at him from beyond the shadows.

Thessan awoke and giggled.

"You're not going to leave," Foler said. "I'll beat you into death first."

Anneka turned her face away from him.

"Filthy swine," Ishbok said, "you're no better than an animal."

Foler lunged at him, but Ishbok stepped to one side, turned and ran out the door into the corridor. Behind him Thessan was shrieking with glee.

Without stopping, Ishbok started to climb the stairway. He went up three stories without stopping.

His heart was pounding wildly when he stopped to listen. An acid taste had come up from his stomach. He threw up a little onto the black finished floor of the landing. He staggered toward the door which led into the city level and looked inside. Dark. He could not see inside.

Suddenly he heard a noise from below. Foler and Thessan were coming up after him. He turned in time to see Foler reach the landing, knife in hand.

Ishbok ran into the darkness of the room. As his eyes adjusted, he saw a door ahead of him, outlined in pale light. When he reached it a dark figure stepped into the frame. Ishbok heard Thessan's idiot laugh echo in the empty room. Somehow Thessan had reached this level by another way. The brothers were playing with him, he realized. He stopped and heard Foler come through the door behind him.

The thought of being beaten by Foler and Thessan was suddenly unbearable. Ishbok rushed toward Thessan's dark form. He bent low and knocked the shadow on its back with his head. The impact sent both of them sliding on the black floor until they came to a stop in the center of the next room.

Here the windows were gray with dawnlight. Ishbok saw another door at the far end as he scrambled to his feet. Thessan was clutching at him and shrieking. Ishbok kicked him in the ribs to free his right foot, and raced across the polished floor, out into the corridor and up the stairs. He heard Foler screaming at Thessan as he climbed, but when he paused on the next landing he heard only his own breathing.

"When I catch you," Foler shouted suddenly, "you'll never lech after a woman again!" His laugh echoed in the stair space.

Ishbok's one hope was to outlast the brothers in the climb. If he could get enough of a lead, then he could hide on one of the levels. They would not be able to guess where he had left the stairs.

He went up two more levels and stopped. Heavy footsteps chattered like curses from below. He took another deep breath and fled up the stairs, trying to step as lightly as possible.

One stretch of stairs, then another, a landing, the next stretch, a new landing, and the next. His bare feet were being burned by the friction of leather in his boots. After half a dozen turns he began to feel pain in his lungs. His heart was going to burst and his eyes would pop out of their sockets; he forced himself to the next landing and stopped.

He filled his lungs with air and held his breath for a few seconds, but the pulse of blood in his ears drowned all sound from below.

Gradually he heard the wheezing and labored breathing of the two men. Foler's curses grew louder, threatening to erupt as visible monstrosities; Thessan's high-pitched shrieks were snakes constricting the physical deformities conjured up in Ishbok's mind by Foler's wrath.

Foler's head appeared as he turned to climb the final stretch of stairs. Ishbok turned to climb higher and slipped on the polished surface before the first step. His forehead hit the fourth stair. He lay stunned, clawing at the railing.

In a moment the brothers were on him, collapsing on top of him in a heap. Foler was cackling. "Hold him down, Thes, then I'll cut it off and throw it down—"

Ishbok punched him in the face, and with a lucky thrust put a finger in Thessan's eye. Then he stood up, picking up the knife Foler had dropped.

As he went up the stairs, Ishbok dropped the knife down the stairwell. He reached the next landing and ran into the empty room. The one beyond it was bright with the orange light of the sun rising through the morning storm clouds. Ishbok passed into a third room. Here the windows were being dotted with the first rain drops of the storm. At the other end of the room he went through a door and found more stairs.

He went down two levels and hid in a windowless chamber. He tried to relax in the dark corner. If they caught up with him again, he would need all his strength. His best hope was that they were now as tired as he was, and would not want to waste the day. There was no food in the upper levels of the city; either Ishbok would come back or starve. If he tried to leave the city, they would be waiting. An upward climb would help him only briefly. Even if he could sneak past them into the countryside, they would track him like an animal. And today they would have food; tomorrow they would have food, while he would be weaker.

After a long while he got up, deciding that he would rather starve and die than be captured for the amusement of Foler and Thessan. They would humiliate him in front of Anneka, maiming and disfiguring him permanently. Then he would never be able to leave the group. He would not be able to hunt. He would grow old exchanging his skills for food and protection. They would force him to teach Anneka's sons. And when he was old and useless and empty of dreams, they would turn him out to die.

Anneka had never loved him; he had proof enough of that. But before he died, he would reach the top of the city. That much he could still accomplish; he would keep faith with his wish of long ago.

He fled upward for most of the morning, stopping to rest in dozens of rooms. The rain stopped and the sun rose with him, looking into the windows, lighting up his way, warming the chill of morning. He would stop occasionally to hear the sound of air coming up the stairwell, the sound of a breathing beast about to be loosed after him. The sight of Anneka with Foler would not fade from behind his eyes. His muscles were tight as he climbed; his mind held a naked hope, almost as if there would be some kind of answer at the top of the city, something so much greater than his life that it would destroy the hurt of the morning. He willed himself upward.

Finally, he came through the opening which led him out onto the flat area behind the great spire. He felt like a wanderer in a dream state. His lungs were heavy, his feet hurt, and he felt dizzy. The sun was hot on his face. It had won the race toward noon. The air was still and hot. He stopped to wipe the sweat off his face with the sleeve of his hide jerkin.

Ahead lay an open plain of metal. On it sat more than thirty aircraft from the old time, huge metallic birds, motionless. He walked toward them slowly, forgetting for a moment the reality of loss behind him.

He stopped beside one of the flying things and pulled himself up inside through an opening. He was inside a bubble-like window. He imagined that the craft was moving through the clouds, carrying him away from the city, freeing him of his prison.

His whole life had been a confinement. He would not have Anneka. There would be no children to weep over his death. He might have told them his dreams. Now there would be nothing.

He looked up at the blue sky. It was a desert of false promises, beckoning him on with unreal suggestions of worlds beyond; there was nothing there that could help him.

As his strength drained away, he sat back in the bubble. The climb had taken all his energy. There was no way to gain it back. Sleep was the only escape.

He woke up choking on the hot air trapped inside the bubble. The afternoon sun was a blinding fire in the sky, rousing him back to the struggle of his life. Death and his brother, sleep, fled before the eye of the sun called Caesar as he scrambled out of the aircraft.

A strong breeze cooled him. Huge clouds sat on the northern horizon, promising a storm by evening.

He walked to the edge of the city and looked out over the countryside of green hills and rocky outcroppings and the blue stream which twisted away to the hazy blue at the end of the world.

He looked down and saw three people moving away from the city. The figures were so small, so insignificant; he felt no interest in them. And he felt no hunger or thirst. His warm body drank the cool wind. He shivered and turned to walk back toward the flying machine. Perhaps he could rest under a wing.

He opened his eyes at night and the infinity of sky and stars had become a cage. The ring was a barrier, saying to him that he had climbed so far and would be permitted to go no higher. This plane of metal would be his grave, guarded by mechanical birds. The wind would blow away his flesh, the sun would bleach his bones; starlight would enter the open eyes of his stony skull to stir whatever ghosts of thought remained. He would lie here forever, as dead as his world, scarcely more dead than the life into which he had been born. Caesar would burn away, the veil of air would be torn from Cleopatra, all the time of passing would dwindle, but he would never come again.

Ishbok closed his eyes, looking for a semblance of peace within himself; now he found only weariness and hunger and hurt. He imagined the black wing of the aircraft moving down to cover him from the cold. Tears forced themselves out through his closed eyelids and he tasted their salt on his lips. The fever shivered his body.

Sleep came gently and he gave himself up to its calm.

III

Once, long ago, when he lay dying, a black dot appeared in the morning sky, growing larger as it came down until he screamed at its closeness. Then it crushed him and he had died.

Something strong held his head; his body was almost unfeeling. He opened his eyes. White, as if the very air were white. Black floaters in his eyes, flowing in and out of his direct vision. *Eye clouds,* his mother had called them, telling him to worry only if he saw one which did not move when he tried to look at it. Good food would always clear them up, and the same ones would not last more than a year.

He remembered light spilling out from an entranceway of some kind, like daylight but stronger, more like the white around him now. A strange thing sitting on the plane of metal . . .

Something was creating images in his brain, pushing him to think, changing him, prodding . . .

A man's garment reminded him of a mirror-wing moth, glittering. He sat in a small vessel, guiding it into a giant ship floating in the dark . . .

Time running backward . . . war fabers marching through snowy passes . . . across green fields . . .

An explosive burst of white light . . .

Plagues . . . piled bodies . . .

A world emptying out, subsiding into a terrible silence . . .

His world.

Reclaimed.

A word referring to him.

Others were being gathered from all over the world.

Slowly, thoughts became words, strange yet clear. Their meaning filled a need in him, one he had felt but never fully understood. Unfolding comprehension was wondrous, and frightening, as if the fiery sun itself were speaking to him.

". . . we have come to rebuild."

Suddenly he was rushing through space toward a yellow sun, and closer to linger over a blue world . . .

"Earth, the original home of your people and mine. The area of space within five hundred light years of Sol is dotted with failed colonies established more than a thousand years ago. Most are lingering near death. Our newest ships will link these worlds into a loose confederation. We have brought tools, generating plants which have the power of small suns. We have synthesis techniques to help you make all that is needed for life."

Ishbok opened his eyes and saw the woman's face. "Why

should you want to do all this?"

"We wish to help," she said. Her hair was white, clinging to her head in short curls; her eyes were green. "A confederation benefits all who belong. It is better to live under law, in social and physical health; a confederation is better than being alone."

Ishbok thought of the food-gathering groups he had known, and how they depended on each other, suffering from need and at each other's hands.

"But why talk with me?"

She smiled. "Because I think you understand, and that will help you lead your people."

"Lead?"

"Rest now. There will be more to learn later." Her face receded into the white and a healing lethargy crept into his eyes, closing them.

He awoke feeling stronger than he had ever remembered; yet there was still a sense of struggle in his mind.

He knew so many new things, puzzling facts which he accepted without hesitation. The white room was in a giant starship circling Cleopatra. The starcrossing vessel was 10 kilometers long and capable of enormous velocities in excess of light speed. The offworlders had rebuilt his health. But he struggled with the thought of a device inside his head. "It will answer questions," the white-haired woman had told him. Answers to any question he might think, as long as there was an answer in the starship's memory elements. He did not always understand the answers. There was a strange new country inside him, as vast as all the libraries he had known, as complete as all the knowledge of humankind, the central homefire of a species.

He tried to sit up and the bed shaped itself to support him.

This new world will always be a part of you now, the woman had said.

Who were these offworlders who could see inside each other? Was it right for anyone to have such power?

"We are your brothers and sisters." The words were inside him, whispering across the presence of knowledge which suddenly seemed a precious gift.

"But that is how you want me to see it!" Ishbok shouted and sat up in his bed.

A door opened in the wall to his left, startling him. The woman with white curls walked in and sat down in the chair next to his bed.

"You've been debating with your tutor-link quite a lot, sometimes even in your sleep." She smiled again. "Let's be friends, Ishbok. My name is Hela Fenn. You can call me Fenn. My profession is psycho-soc. Do you have another name?"

Ishbok noted that she had known his name, but he did not remember giving it to her. "It's the only one," he said, wondering how much of himself was no longer his own.

"How's your understanding of incoming material? Do you get a full picture of why we are here?"

Ishbok nodded. "How old are you, Fenn?"

"I'm forty."

Almost twice Anneka's age, older in Earth years. Older than anyone he had ever known.

"Everything we've learned about you, Ishbok, indicates strong mental abilities in a number of directions. You understand alternatives quickly, you know how much you can do and not do with the resources at hand; you will lead if given the chance, but you are willing to follow if you agree with one who leads—"

"How can you know these things? I don't even know them—"

"By your responses to dream strategies."

Ishbok felt a moment of fear.

"It's perfectly safe. Just like dreaming, except that certain decisive patterns are brought forward and reinforced."

"I don't like it and I don't want it ever again. And I don't know if I believe what you say about this tutor in my head. It seems to me that you may have the power to control my actions."

"Good," she said. "You're showing aggressively rational behavior. You'll need it to help your world."

He was about to object again, but he understood her.

"If you like," she said, "we can remove the link and give you an external head band—but that might be inconvenient. You might not have benefit when you most need it."

"Perhaps."

"Get dressed and we'll go to the observation deck. Later we'll shuttle down to your city and get you started."

"You make it sound easy."

"Only the travel part, Ishbok," she said as she stood up. "The rest will be difficult, and you may fail." She turned and went out through the opening door, leaving him with a feeling of suspicion and apprehension.

Ishbok looked out into night and stars. Cleopatra glowed in blues and golds and browns, veiled in silvery clouds, encircled by the diamond dust of the ring, faceted debris and sculpted Moons. Screens in back of him let in the light of Caesar; others showed space in various directions from the starship.

My world, he thought. *Nowhere is its suffering visible.*

"I'm sorry to be late," Hela Fenn said. He turned around as she was sitting down in one of the lounge chairs. She pointed to a seat opposite her own and put one foot up on the low table in the middle. "Sit down, Ishbok."

He noticed her clothes for the first time. One-piece green suit, wide pants, half boots. The garment came up around her neck in a tight fit.

"Do you really care?" he asked as he sat down.

"How do you mean?"

"My world—do you really care about helping?"

"I could give you a purely emotional answer which might please, but that would be to go against my convictions. Yes, we care, but we will all gain economically and socially. We are all Earth peoples. More than a thousand years ago, the home planet cast off its innovators, malcontents, idealists, dreamers—whatever name can be attached to them. A period of turmoil and cultural sterility followed, one which is not yet completely over. And this decline was mirrored in the history of every colony world we have visited. The colonists took bits and pieces of Earth with them, including all the old problems, and it shows in the state of every colony world we've seen.

"As nearly as we can make out from a year of investigation, the following is what happened on Cleopatra since the arrival of humankind more than a thousand years ago. A world grew in all directions from the place of landing. People grew different from one another; they moved away to create different places. The world filled up. Cleopatra changed. The local flora and fauna retreated before the life from Earth." She paused for a moment. "It's been coming back recently, but the world is a hybrid. Two kinds of fabers exist now, where once there was only one. At first fabers were modified to be workers and servants, and performers—dancers, musicians; they were also research animals. The warlike fabers hunt the original fabers, and men hunt them both.

"Anyway, the emerging nations grew apart. There were small wars and large wars; eventually a few small nations dragged Dardania and Pindaria, the largest powers, into a war involving biological weapons. It ended with a nuclear holocaust. The only good thing about the use of atomic weapons in those final days was that their use was confined to a few large cities and against military bases."

It's going to start all over, he thought, *unless we could become . . . something else, perhaps something that did not live on worlds where even simple things were lacking . . .*

". . . but enough has remained to start again."

"This ship is almost a small world, isn't it, Fenn?"

"You can think of it that way. It's as large as many cities were in the past, in the centuries before space travel."

He looked directly at her for a moment.

"Is anything the matter, Ishbok?" Her look was helpful, serious, without guile.

"I'm wondering about what I have come to, if it is possible for me to be right."

"You're one of the ones Cleopatra needs." She spoke without a trace of hesitation.

"Why are you so sure—what do you know that I can't see?"

"I see what you will see when you find yourself in the reality of leading. You will know what to do, or you will not."

He stood up and turned away from her to look at the sight of Cleopatra. *They are all planning this,* he thought. *They think I will inevitably choose what they will agree with. What if I do things they cannot support? Surely they must know*

I am having doubts? Still, I cannot let the chance pass to stand between my people and these offworlders. I cannot let so much opportunity go by. She's right. I can help.

He looked at the planet swimming in the starry void. *To them my world is an island.*

"I'll be with you to help, Ishbok," Hela Fenn said behind him. "I know what you must be feeling."

You may know too much, he thought. He wondered if they were capable of killing him; or if they were truly so wise as to know all the needs of his world, and his own.

He noticed then that she was standing next to him. There was a restrained pride in her stance, unlike anything he had ever seen in another person.

"If it will help you to know," she said, "there are those on Earth who oppose all the help we are trying to administer among the failing colonies. Our compromise with them is to let native leaders take the major role, whenever we can. To do nothing would be cruelty, don't you think?"

"I feel hopeful about what you say," he said, "but I must see more." *My world, my world, I pledge myself to you. I will do the best I know how, the best I can learn . . .*

"To be honest," she said, "there is some vanity in it."

Swirling clouds rushed up at the shuttle, replacing the sight of oceans and land with obscurity. *To come back and be so close,* he thought, *makes my world all the universe there is again.* He sat watching the forward screen in the passenger section of the shuttle. Hela Fenn sat next to him.

Soon the clouds broke and he saw the landing area of the city far below. The city grew larger.

"There will be a crowd," Hela Fenn said. "You know what to expect?"

"Yes."

"We're drifting down on gravs now. Try and smile when the crowd cheers. It's important to have them like you. Almost a quarter of all remaining human life has been gathered into this city since you've been gone. Do you feel the role you will play, my friend? Can you see your children and their future?"

He felt alone. "What will come must be better than what I grew up in." The crowd was looking up at him through the screen. The old air machines were gone, cleared by the offworlders. He missed the old hulks.

The shadow of the circular shuttle grew smaller on the landing surface. The screen went dark as they touched, but went on again to show faces peering into the passenger section. Ishbok noted that they were mostly young faces—men and women looking newly washed and fed, and cautious in their expressions.

Hela Fenn led the way out between the empty seats. Ishbok followed her to the center of the cabin. They stood together on the lift plate which dropped them down into the airlock.

The lock was already open, the oval exit framing the crowd outside. Hela stepped out first. Ishbok followed and stood next to her at the top of the ramp. The shuttle was a ceiling above them, casting a shadowy circle. Beyond the circle the crowd stood in Caesar's light.

Ishbok searched the faces of the closest ones, the unfamiliar faces filled with hope.

"One of your own!" Hela said, her voice booming from amplification and bouncing in the space under the shuttle. "He knows what Cleopatra needs; he knows what you need; he knows what the city needs. He will carry our help to you. Go to him, talk with him, tell him what can be done."

The crowd cheered. The sunlight seemed brighter.

"Soon the city's water, heat and light will be working fully. You will be able to farm the countryside; and later we will show you how to live without agriculture. These are material things only. Your task will be to educate yourselves, administer laws, reconciling all the differences between yourselves, the process which makes a state necessary." She stopped speaking. "Now, let's go down among them," she whispered.

Anneka's face caught him from the center of the crowd. He stood frozen, afraid, naked in his new clothes. Then he noticed Foler and Thessan standing next to her. *They don't recognize me,* he thought. Anneka seemed bewildered.

"We'll go through the crowd and down to your office and living quarters a floor below," Hela whispered. "You must go first."

Ishbok walked down the ramp, all the while staring at Anneka. When he reached the bottom of the ramp, he was too low to see her in the throng. Fenn was next to him. They walked forward.

The cheering resumed as the crowd parted for him. He walked ahead trying to smile as hands grasped at him and slapped his shoulders.

A man stepped in front of him. Ishbok recognized Foler—cleaner, shaved, dressed in offworlder fabrics, he was still surviving in his own way.

"What did you have to do to get all this, fool?"

You'll be opening a new period of history. The words chased each other through his brain. *Cleopatra will become a crossroads of interstellar commerce and cultural exchange.*

"You had better step aside," Hela Fenn said. "If this crowd hears you they'll tear you apart. Back off."

Foler stepped aside, his face mocking them. Ishbok hurried past him, through the rest of the crowd, and down a half-familiar flight of stairs. Hela Fenn was at his side as they came out into a lighted passage.

She walked ahead of him down the corridor, past one open door after another. Ishbok glimpsed workmen rebuilding the interiors. She stopped in front of a large door at the end. It slid open and he followed her inside.

"This is where you will live and work." The room was carpeted in soft green. A desk stood in the alcove of three windows, giving him an unobstructed view of the surrounding countryside.

"Come, sit down behind your desk," she said. She sat down in one of the chairs facing it. He sat down and looked at her.

"We're an empty world," he said, "which might be turned to advantages I can't guess yet."

"I picked you as one who would question and object," she said.

"On the way down you were telling me about history. Could you continue, Hela? I was very interested."

"I was talking about the need to break out of the cycles of prosperity and decline—the general rule among civilizations, at least the human ones we've seen."

"Are there others?"

"We don't know yet, but we're sure there are. Anyway, part of the answer lies in the use of vast resources, far beyond the kind available on a single planet. A single solar system is a good industrial base. The struggle then passes from a filling of material needs to a development of internal resources, the inner satisfactions of a human being. That part we don't fully understand yet. What we are fairly certain of is that there is no absolute necessity for the rise and decline of cultures. There may be a way out."

"What if you're wrong? What if it's always birth, decay, death, and new beginnings? I see it in the man who stopped me outside, Foler."

"The new courts will deal with him."

"Can the courts take away his hatred of me? Can they remove his desire to mutilate me with a knife?"

Ishbok saw the pained expression on Hela's face. "I know you've seen a lot of darkness. But the light is there. We have to try."

Ishbok wondered if Anneka had gone to Foler out of choice, or to save the blademaker's life. Perhaps Foler had told her to play up to him so he would keep on producing tools; perhaps she even loved Foler.

"We're hoping that those like yourself, Ishbok, will have enough internal resources to resist decline."

"I cannot live forever. The time of those like Foler will come again." He smiled at her, feeling his own bitterness. "But I will try, Hela, I will try." *Anneka, did you save my life, even once?*

"Later . . . we'll send you a few security experts, Ishbok. They will help you train your own police force. There will also be experts who will help you run the city, including the schools, which will help create your own teams."

"Will my police carry weapons?"

"Harmless ones—the kind that can stop but not kill." She paused. "You will have enemies. The power will be yours to use. You will have to control it."

He saw Foler with a spear in his chest. Thessan hurtling to his death from the top of the city.

"I'm afraid of my thoughts, Hela, maybe you were wrong about me."

"If anything you convince me more. You're a kind, concerned man, one who would never seek power; therefore you are the one who must use it. You will form a government and you will govern."

Suddenly the words ran out between them. *I can never be one of the offworlders,* his thoughts continued. *I've never belonged to any of the groups I've known. I've always been alone, holding back.* The awkward silence was a prison, an equilibrium of agreement and disagreement between Hela and himself. *And I am not completely a Cleopatran either.*

As if in answer, Hela Fenn said, "You will be the first of the new Cleopatrans. Let me tell you the story of Cincinnatus the Roman . . ."

IV

In the first months of mayorship, the representatives of the various groups gathering in the city came to talk with him; the captain of the starship paid a call, as did many volunteers from Earth. The representatives confused him; the captain made him suspicious; the volunteers brought the skills he needed, so he put them to work. There were so many details in the doing of things that he almost forgot who he was.

"Leadership is being the center of a storm," Hela said in the second month. He was more interested in getting things done than in theorizing about them. There was more worry in thoughts than he could carry from day to day.

In the third month Foler raped one of the women volunteers from the starship, a medic. He held his own brother as a hostage to avoid capture by the police, and killed Thessan before surrendering. The trial which Ishbok had thought could be avoided was held. He did not attend and refused to have anything to do with it, although he might have been one of the three judges who heard the case.

"He grew up surviving," Hela had said to him. "He knows no other life and never will. His sense of inadequacy is complete in the new way of things, where nothing is open to him through the cruel means he knew in the past."

"I did not learn those ways."

"Your parents, Ishbok."

He sighed. "What will be the sentence?"

"We can retrain him, wipe memories, initiate new behavior and value patterns."

"You might just as well kill him—it's the same when you take away identity and memory."

"You could imprison him, or kill him instead. We'll do what we know how only with your permission, and if the court agrees."

"I don't know, Hela, I'll have to think." *Kill him! He's hopeless.*

"Let the courts decide," she said, "you're too close. If your courts don't have this power of decision, you'll have a world of power by individuals with no reference to laws."

The conversation had made him angry. The remembered rigmarole had not resulted in a solution for him. In a moment Anneka would come into his office. She was four months pregnant with Foler's child.

The door slid open. She came in and sat down in the chair in front of the desk. "I've come," she said, "to ask you not to kill Foler."

"I've made no plans to kill him, Anneka." *Anneka,* his thoughts whispered softly.

"And I want you to understand, more than anything," she continued without looking at him. "I chose him because I love him. But I would have chosen him anyway, because he was strong and would protect our children." She looked at him with tears in her eyes. "You are for another world. I tried to attract you so you would stay and make knives and points—I like you, but not as a lover or a father. I'm sorry, but don't kill him. I won't know what to say to his son."

"What if it's a daughter?"

"It will be a son," she said. A world of brutality stood behind her words, all of Foler's defiance and will, and she still lived in its service. *I could not be a father to her children,* Ishbok thought, *but I can be a protector of my city and my world.*

"He may not die, Anneka, but he may return . . . changed. It will not be my decision, but the court's."

She looked at him with doubt. "You let others make your choices—how can you be a man?"

"Don't you see, the same law must apply to all. I cannot decide. If I do, it will be meddling." *I'm not really sure,* he thought, *but I must decide.*

She stood up with restrained hatred in her eyes and spit at his desk.

She came to manipulate me again, he thought as Anneka turned and went out. The door slid shut and he sat in the silence of the room, listening to the sound of his pulse pounding in his ears, marking his own rising hatred, not only of Anneka and Foler, but of everything from which he had sprung.

The sooner it was swept away the better . . .

In the evening Ishbok was alone in the silence of the blood-red sun. He looked out across the valley at the deep blue shadows cast by the setting sun, and wondered about the future.

He tried to imagine this confederation, this greater world into which his wayside world would emerge. What battles, what disagreements would be possible there? What cycles of birth, decay and death, and new beginnings lay ahead for a civilization spanning the stars? How many isolate worlds were there tucked away in the miserable corners of the universe? He wondered if Cleopatra had better been left unfound, lost among the grains of stars, to rebuild by itself from its family squabbles rather than be shamed by intruders from the stars.

But he knew that it would be impossible now for him to see Cleopatra as the whole world; he had seen his home from beyond the sky, a glowing sphere set in a night of stars. He had seen its oceans, its land, the ring sweeping around the planet like unwanted riches being cast off into the void. He had looked down into the dark hemisphere where this city lay, invisible; he had seen it light up in the night, coming back to life after a thousand years.

Cleopatra circled Caesar, and Caesar was only one star among a countless number, yet all the importance of his life lay here. His own people would mistrust him, and he would mistrust the offworlders; there was no safety in the thought. He would not be able to forget all that was; he would do his best to affect what would be.

Now he would have to be more than a warrior or a hunter or a craftsman, or a father; he would have to be a ruler, a helper.

The sun slid halfway behind the horizon. *I will have to learn to speak to my own people, as well as I speak with Hela. My children will have to know more than I do.* He thought of the many world histories belonging to the other worlds of the sky. He would ask Hela for them. Maybe there would be something he could learn from such a study. There were other reclaimed worlds entering the confederation. He tried to picture new, unspoiled worlds circling distant suns . . .

He thought of Anneka and her child. He wondered how

the city would react to Foler's coming sentence, whatever that would be.

The sun was down. Stars appeared in the sky. Below him city light spilled out into the valley. The ring cut a swath in the sky, a carpet preparing the way for chunky Charmian to rise and overtake Iras. Clouds sat on the northern horizon, promising a storm by morning. A black-winged deltasoar sailed into the twilight.

Ishbok stood up, sighing, knowing what he would do. He would govern with all the help there was to be had. He had become someone else, a stranger who would daily startle his earlier self; there was terror in the thought.

He knew that he would be lonely.

In the Distance, and Ahead in Time

"And openly I pledged my heart to the grave and suffering land, and often in the consecrated night, I promised to love her faithfully until death, unafraid, with her heavy burden of fatality, and never to despise a single one of her enigmas. Thus did I join myself to her with a mortal cord."

—*Holderlin,*
The Death of Empedocles

"How big did they say it is?" Alan asked as he looked up at the new star in the night sky.

"Fifty klicks across," Gemma said, feeling the wonder of it take hold of her again. "A whole city wrapped around an asteroid core! Just think, Alan, they're people from Old Earth, like us. They'll help us."

"No." He shook his head. "Not like us at all, so why should they help us?"

Her brother's disapproval of her reaction to the visit worried her, but she was sure he would change his mind when he understood how the habitat would benefit the colony.

"What kind of people lock themselves up like that," he went on contemptuously, "hiding themselves away from sunlight, generation after generation?"

"It's not like that at all," Gemma said softly. "The number of shells going down to the asteroid core must give them at least half the land area of a planet the size of Earth, and all of it usable."

"Really? How would you know that?"

"Just calculate the area of the inside surface of a sphere and multiply that by the number of shells within shells, allowing for decrease in size toward the core."

She couldn't see his face clearly in the starlight, but knew that he was looking at her with that slightly contemptuous look he put on whenever she knew something he didn't. "And I suppose you'll tell me they farm it," he said.

"They have what farms do."

"What do you know about it?"

"It's all in the history books," she replied, and listened to the awkward silence that was his frequent way of reproaching her. You could be doing more work around the farm, instead of wasting your time reading old books. He did not have to say it. She felt a twinge whenever she thought about the fragility of images stored in the old hand-held readers. The only reason they had lasted this long was that very few people wanted to read what was in them.

They watched their world's rotation carry the visitor below the mountainous horizon, then strolled back toward the farmhouse, which always seemed to be waiting for them, its lone porch lamp pale yellow in the darkness. The glow of the neighboring house, three kilometers south across the plateau, winked out early, probably to save the aging wind generator. Nina Stroeve and her brothers always went to sleep at the same hour. Cyril, her younger brother, was always the first one up, but Nathaniel, the stepbrother, often got to work very late in the morning. Gemma felt a chill, and wondered again if the climate on the plateau was changing faster than expected.

She knew enough about the land to feel insecure. The fertile plateau would one day crumble to the level of the forest that surrounded it on three sides, as its substructure was eroded by underground streams from the mountains in the north. That would eventually cut off the colony's one hundred square kilometers from the flow of water, turning the plateau into another of the islands that towered over the jungle. She had studied these isolated cakes of land through binoculars, and had concluded that only the ever-weakening bridge to the mountains was delaying the colony's fate. The plateau's geologic fate was to become part of the rich forest that crowded around it: and it was the colony's future to grow and go down into the forest, and really begin to settle the planet. It might take a century or more, once the forest was mapped and its dangers discovered. The greatest danger to the colony would be to cling to the plateau. But whenever she discussed this with Alan, the other farmers, or the mayor of the town, they smiled and said that the problem was too far ahead in time to take seriously. The plateau might stand for a thousand years, which was true, of course; or there might be landslides within a few years.

Years ago, she had noticed within herself and in others an uneasiness about settling the forest, more than a consideration of difficulties or mere reluctance to leave the plateau.

They came to the porch steps and sat down. "What do they want here?" Alan asked uneasily. "What right do they have to disturb us?"

"I think they're curious about others of their own kind."

"I know you're excited, but I wish they'd mind their own business."

Again, she felt disappointed by his disparaging tone and lack of interest, but did not answer.

"I guess I never imagined that we'd meet people from the mobiles, or from anywhere else but here. Who would've thought it?"

"Well, now we'll have to think about it," she said as gently as possible.

"I wish they hadn't come."

Gemma felt resentful, because there were too many things Alan didn't want to think about. Now he knew that he might have to start, but was still resisting stubbornly. He never asked why they were still up here on the plateau, nearly a century after the colony had been founded. Sure, everyone was comfortable, so much so that they avoided facing the possibility that human beings might never be able to fit in elsewhere on this world. She had discussed the problem with Paul Beares, one of the medical doctors in town. He had admitted that it might be a problem, but not something that anyone alive now would have to deal with. On the plateau, the colonists had been able to impose their own biology and farm the land. But if they tried to live in the teeming forest below, or elsewhere on the planet, they would have to face the bacterial and viral life, something for which their limited medical science was not prepared. Long-term survival required that the growing population, now at nearly ten thousand, leave the plateau; but the planet's biology might be too complex to fight, and the colony's isolation had only slowed learning more about the planet.

It might have been different if the old starship had survived. Its teaching programs would have been the basis of a growing educational system that would have helped needed technologies survive into the present. Their loss had only encouraged the preachers who had always condemned the dangerous accomplishments of the past, solidifying the bare, stoic religiosity by which the colonists came to accept their lot.

It had cost their grandparents dearly to come here, but they had been eager to leave the ruined solar system, with its dead Earth and dead Mars, to find open air and sky. The rest of this world might be dangerous, but they had been able to sterilize the plateau and start up their farms on it. There had been no choice for the first settlers. The starship could never have been a home; but life on the plateau became clearly defined, and they could console themselves with the hope that their descendants would one day spread across the planet.

But the plateau was only a fragile piece of soft land jutting out from the mountains, sediment that was slowly being eaten away by the jungle to the south and eroded by water from the north. It had been breaking off into the forest for ages, like a glacier into the sea. Some of the original accounts and observations, still available in the town library, had described this whole region as having once been sea bottom. Currents had filled in a vast area with sediment, and when the ocean had receded, the built-up land had begun to erode and collapse, creating the cakelike plateaus.

The largest area of sediment was here, up against the mountains; it was breaking off to the south at more than a meter per year, as well as being eroded by underground streams from the north. She had been able to measure this much by herself, for five years now. What she could not measure was the underground erosion that was weakening the entire plateau. The community's reluctance about even sending out survey teams to assess the difficulties of founding another colony was based on the fear of disease, which might be passed between the two communities years later, even if survey teams brought back no obvious infection. If a second colony was to be founded, it would have to remain isolated indefinitely.

She was proud of what she had learned by observation, more so than what she had learned at the library; but this year, the large cracks she had found more than three kilometers from the plateau's edge had frightened her. The fissures were widening, and might reach the mountains in less than a century.

Alan's answer to her predictions was to insist that the plateau could easily last for a thousand years or more, and by then a hundred other colonies would be thriving. The mayor had sent out a few people to look at the cracks, but no one knew enough to examine them correctly. Even her own studies were questionable, since she was self-taught. New knowledge was feared, and its absence used to dismiss fear. To deny the colony's dream, to say that it might one day vanish, was more than many people could face. Land breaking off to the south at a meter per year was nothing to fear, they told themselves; fissures three klicks long were as big as they'd ever get.

Alan got up and said, "I'll turn on the lights for you." He started into the house, but paused and glanced up at the stars. "Maybe these visitors will bring us enough biology and medicine to help us settle the forest."

She didn't answer, even though she knew he was trying to admit something of what she had insisted on in their arguments and discussions.

"Well, it's a constructive thought," he continued. "If they can move their world around, they must know a thing or two. Why shouldn't they help us out?"

"Maybe they will," she said, trying to sound agreeable.

"Well," he said, "I'd better get some sleep. Got to fix the tractor and plow the north field before noon, and you've got to start the vegetable preserves."

"Yes," she said, sighing, thinking of how many chickens she had killed in her lifetime, and whether to tell him that the well pipe was clogging up just below the kitchen sink, and that maybe the pump itself wasn't in such good shape either. He had promised to make a better cover for the compost heap, but had never gotten around to it, and the smell didn't seem to bother him.

He paused in front of the door. "What is it?" she asked.

"I wonder why they're *really* here," he said.

2

It was just past noon when Alan got up from his lunch to get another cup of herb tea. Gemma was still sipping hers, waiting to see if he would turn on the radio.

"I haven't forgotten," he said as he switched it on, sat down across from her at the table, and smiled uneasily. He already seemed tired from his morning's work.

"All of us here at the town meeting," Mayor Overton was saying, "and those listening at home, welcome you to our community. Most are at work, so only a few of us are here in the hall, but I assure you we are all very curious about your . . . mobile's visit to our world. You told me earlier that you had come to discuss some very important matters with us."

As usual, the Mayor sounded a bit pompous, but Gemma noticed that he also sounded unusually nervous.

"We do have much to discuss," the offworlder said in a voice that might belong to a man or woman. "I would first like to ask whether my use of your language is clear to you."

"Strange accent," Alan said, leaning over and turning up the volume.

"Perfectly fine," said the Mayor. "Please continue."

"What happened to your starship?"

The Mayor took an audible deep breath and replied,

"When our grandparents came out of cold sleep, they found their automatic ship in a shallow orbit around this planet. Their three shuttles barely had enough time to land people and supplies on this plateau before the orbit decayed and the starship entered the atmosphere. Efforts were made to use the ship's reaction engines to raise its orbit as the shuttles went back and forth, but time ran out. Some of the passengers had taken too long coming out of cold sleep, and had to be left behind. Those who escaped were fortunate, but we still lack far too much."

The last part of the Mayor's statement and his critical tone surprised Gemma, raising her estimation of him. He was alluding to the fact that the colony was founded by people who wanted less, and thought it the better way, using the example of Earth's destruction as justification.

She expected the visitor to ask why there were no video communications, only radio. "We've seen the crater where the starship struck," the offworlder said. "It was a great disaster for the life there."

"We've never seen it," Overton replied impatiently. "Too far away. Our shuttles were out of fuel by the time we got everyone down to the planet. What is it that you wish to say to us?"

There was a long pause. Gemma heard the Mayor shifting in his chair. She got up and opened the kitchen window to let out the heat that had built up from the morning sunlight.

"In the three generations of your life on this world," the offworlder said, "have you ever seen anything of the life in the forest?"

"Well, we do keep to the plateau," the Mayor replied. "It's large enough for us. Some of us have observed the forest with field glasses, but we're too busy to explore, and the climb would be difficult. Besides, it may be dangerous. Diseases might be brought back. We just don't know enough. There are stories of four-footed creatures that occasionally stand up on their hind legs, but from the few reports it seems they don't approach the plateau. I should point out that the clay cliffs are very sheer and nearly impossible to climb from below. We're isolated."

"You think that's a good thing?" the offworlder asked.

"Yes. There's scarcely ten thousand of us. We're not ready for the rest of this world."

"But you will be one day?"

"Someday," the Mayor said. "Why do you ask?"

"Until now," the visitor said, "your presence has not altered the planet. Before that happens, we would like to persuade you to abandon this colony and come live with us. You're welcome to join our world, or build a mobile of your own. We can offer you more than you can imagine."

"What?" Alan shouted, nearly dropping his cup.

Gemma felt a rush of excitement as she understood why the mobile was here.

"Why?" the Mayor asked, his voice rising. "We're content here." Gemma could almost see the bewilderment on his pudgy face as sounds of surprise filled the town hall.

"It's ridiculous!" someone shouted.

"Exactly," Alan said, shaking his head and smiling, but when she caught his eye, she saw that he felt threatened and confused.

"Planets should not be invaded," the offworlder said. "They have their own lives to fulfill."

"What are you saying?" Mayor Overton demanded.

"Surely it's occurred to some of you that you're invaders. While we were nearby, it seemed to some of us that we might discuss this problem with you."

"Problem?" the Mayor replied. "What problem?"

"What will happen to this world's intelligent life."

"But there's none to speak of."

The hall suddenly became quiet. Gemma was taken aback by the point: intelligent life might one day develop on this world, but its rise would be cut short when the colony expanded from the plateau. That was what the offworlder was saying, and with disapproval. She had thought about it, but never as a crime waiting to happen.

Mayor Overton coughed. "Who are you to come here and lecture us about our life?" He sounded more forceful now. "Oh, I get your point well enough, and it may even be true. But as I've told you, our grandparents had to land or die with the incoming ship. We earn our right to life here every day."

The visitor asked, "And it does not disturb you that you may preempt intelligence here?"

"Why should it?" a man shouted from the audience.

"It's Nathaniel," Gemma whispered, realizing why she hadn't seen him coming out of his house late this morning. Then she heard a sound behind her and turned to see Nathaniel's stepbrother Cyril leaning over the open top half of the kitchen door, smiling at her in his usual, inviting way. Gemma usually tolerated his appearing at her door, as though he had a right to stop by at any time, but was suddenly annoyed with him, and looked away.

"Yeah," Cyril said, smoothing back his unruly brown hair. "He should be home helping Nina and me, if he's so devoted to her, but he had to go. They had an argument this morning. Maybe he should move to town permanently and become a schoolster."

"Quiet!" Alan shouted. "I want to hear this."

". . . but we can offer you a choice," the offworlder was

saying, "so you don't have to stay here. Even if you were only to affect the development of simpler bioforms here, that would delay or prevent the emergence of intelligence."

"Our presence here can't be worse than the workings of chance," the Mayor objected. "All life competes with other life."

"But shouldn't each world have the chance to grow in its own way? Something unique may develop here—one way with your presence and another without it. We think you should consider leaving while there is still time. If you stay, you or your descendants may be taking a world away from its people before—"

"Who do you think you are," Nathaniel shouted, "coming here and talking to us as if we were children!"

Gemma glanced at her brother and saw him clench his jaw as he listened to Nathaniel, and she knew that he was thinking of all the work he had put into the farm, of how their parents and grandparents had lived and died to earn every square meter of this land. It was bad enough that she talked about the dangers to the plateau's geology. Now some intruder was telling him to clear off. For her, the offworlder's words suddenly offered escape from the past; for Alan, they called for an end to his way of life. She looked over at Cyril, who seemed surprised by Nathaniel's outburst.

"Are you threatening us?" the Mayor asked.

"Not at all," the visitor said. "Please don't misunderstand. Our aim is to persuade. To help you decide what you think, we will examine the planet for signs of intelligent life."

Gemma heard the Mayor sigh with relief. "Explore all you like. We can't stop you, obviously, but we would prefer to be left in peace."

"What kind of alternative to our life here can you offer us?" a woman asked.

"Besides the chance to join our habitat," the visitor said, "we would provide a habitat shell for you to fill in. We would place it in high planetary orbit and ferry people up. You could perfect it at your leisure."

"You assume," Nathaniel said, "that we would want your way of life," but Gemma had a sudden feeling from the tone of his voice that Nathaniel was curious about the offworlder's way of life.

"No," the offworlder replied, "the habitat would contain your way of life, whatever you would wish to make of it."

"I find that hard to believe. How could we think of abandoning our hard-won place here?"

"Our purpose," the offworlder continued calmly, "is not to dictate to you. We hope that once you have considered the dilemma, you will let this planet develop in its own way—it's your entire colony against the future of perhaps more than one intelligent species."

"Oh, come now," the Mayor said. "How do you know that our descendants might not get along just fine with an emerging native life?"

"It would never get to that point. You're isolated for now, but the expansion of your population and the pressure of various natural changes will drive you from this plateau, and you will be forced to take what you need to survive."

"Your effrontery is unbelievable! You talk as if our staying here were open to debate. It's not and never will be."

"We only present choices and their consequences," the visitor said. "We do not believe in any absolute system of ethical norms, or their enforcement. There are only laws that rise up to serve the needs of a community, and they are not arbitrary if they accomplish that end, however self-serving they may seem to outsiders. Our laws do not govern you. You can still have your own ways when you leave here, and with greater security and power over your own destiny."

"And without any guilt, I suppose," the Mayor said mockingly. "If you're so interested in our welfare, then give us the means to leave the plateau before it's washed away from beneath us."

"That," the offworlder said, "would arm you with the means for a massive assault on the planet's ecology. Every microorganism and animal that you deemed dangerous to your life would eventually die, and the effects would become irreversible."

Gemma noticed that Alan was staring at the radio as if at an enemy. The Mayor had publicly admitted the danger to the plateau, and that the only solution would be to abandon it, something that Alan had never quite believed. She glanced toward Cyril. He also seemed a bit worried, but gave her a puzzled smile, shifting his weight as he leaned on the bottom half of the door.

"Well," the Mayor said finally. "Do you have anything else to say to us?"

"No, but thank you for listening. You may not understand yet, but we are ready to give you all the help you need to remake your lives."

"As long as we leave the planet?"

"Yes."

Alan got up from the table, opened the bottom part of the kitchen door, and pushed past Cyril. Gemma got up, went after him, and sat down at his left on the back steps. Without a word, Cyril came over and sat down next to her.

Alan said, "They just show up out of nowhere and tell us to leave the planet. Are they insane?"

"They're concerned about us," Gemma said.

"It's not their business what we do here. All life struggles, and there's no way to know what will survive. An asteroid might strike tomorrow and wipe us all out. We have as much right to be here as anywhere else."

"But shouldn't we look ahead?"

"You want to believe there's something to all this," he said, "because you never cared about our place here. I don't care what happens a million years from now."

She tried to ignore his reproach. But he was right, as far as it went. What could she look forward to here? If Alan married Nina, then Nina would move into this house. Gemma liked Cyril well enough but it was not love and Nathaniel had never shown any interest in her. Marriage to either of them would only mean trading places with Nina. Alan wanted her to find someone she could bring here and have children with, to benefit the farm. It would have to be someone who did not have a farm. And she suspected that he wanted her to stay with him for as long as possible, but was hiding the attachment he felt, which had grown stronger after the influenza that had killed their parents.

She took his arm and asked, "But what if it's much sooner than that? What if there is intelligent life here now?"

He pushed her arm away. "No one has a right to tell me where to live. Let them look. They won't find anything. We're the only ones here."

"I'll see you folks later," Cyril said as he stood up, looking pale and uneasy. "Got work to do." He walked away and started down the road toward his farm.

"Sorry!" Alan called out after him. "Tell Nina I'll be over as soon as I can."

"You'd better!" Cyril shouted without looking back, then raised a hand in farewell and kept walking.

Puzzled for a moment by Cyril's behavior, Gemma held

Alan's arm in silence, then said, "Don't you see that we live here in a kind of deliberate backwardness?"

"Backwardness?" he asked, looking at the ground.

"We could have so much more if we had not rejected so much of the past."

"It was a betterment," Alan said.

"No, no," she replied, taking his arm again. "We're hiding here, living within narrow, precarious limits."

"Earth died," he replied bitterly, but without pushing her away this time, "by breaking all natural limits. I never want my life to change, or that of my children. I want it whole, as it is. We should have destroyed those old readers a long time ago." His voice broke as he was overcome by his feelings, and she realized how deeply he felt that any change was his enemy.

"I sometimes go and look out at the forests," she said softly, "and I can't help feeling that we're hiding up here. Did you ever wonder why we don't go exploring?"

"It's dangerous to our health."

"Yes, so we burned the life here to make a place for ourselves. It's not our world, Alan, because we had to do that. We came here to be free, but we're still afraid, and we cling to each other." And you cling too much to me, she had almost said.

He turned and looked at her. "You don't even sound like one of us. We're all a problem to you. I'm a problem to you, it's as if you grew up elsewhere."

She let go of his arm. "I've read and I've thought for myself, Alan. I'm not blind."

"And I am?"

"You feel a lot, but you refuse to think."

"What's there to think about? We're here, on land we paid for with two generations, and continue to pay for with our work, with our whole lives."

"And that gives us the right to expand?"

"Yes, when the time comes!"

"Even if it means preventing the intelligent life that might grow here one day? Alan, don't you see? We might prevent it without ever knowing!"

He looked at her with dismay, and for the first time she saw hatred crowding out the fear in his brown eyes. "I don't care. We can't be responsible for mere possibilities. It's only a lot of talk going on as if it were real."

"We should be thinking," she said softly, "about what we've been avoiding for a long time. It was understandable when we had to live here, but now we have a choice."

He stood up and glared down at her, then marched away toward the tractor in the north field. She watched him for a while, feeling numb, then got up and went back into the kitchen.

As she washed the dishes from lunch, she looked out the window and tried to understand her brother's feelings. Alan cared more about the farm than she did, and everything he had said was based on his feelings for the place. He had imagined himself secure here on the plateau until the facts about the coming erosion had started coming out; but he had been able to set that aside, as a problem that was at least a century or more away. The whole colony was like Alan, she realized, afraid of the silent questions posed by the world around it. The mobile was only the voice of deeply held fears and doubts reminding the colony of how much it had failed.

She wondered what Nathaniel must be feeling now. He had dreamed of exploring this world one day. "It will all be ours," he had once told her confidently.

She dried her hands and sat down again at the table determined to make things clear to herself. The new thoughts brought by the offworlders mobile faced the colony with a frightening choice, greater than any of its old problems, and she was suddenly glad that the colony had not looked for heavy metals in the mountains and developed industrial skills, or pursued biomedical research, because then it would have forgotten its fear of the past, abandoned its modest way of life, and invaded the forest.

Feeling lonely and conflicted she got up and tried to decide what to cook for dinner. The beans would have to be soaked and then simmered until dark to be ready on time, and she would have to kill a chicken, decide how to cook it, and maybe get some three-bean salad preserves from the pantry. As she started to organize the ingredients, the tractor started with a series of sputtering coughs, and died. Alan would not be able to finish the north field's plowing today unless he fixed it.

She sat down again at the table, feeling Alan's defeat by the tractor merge with his fears about the future and thought about calling Nina on the radio for a talk, but decided against it. Nina might not want to talk after arguing with her brother; Cyril was sure to be after her about when she was going to settle down with Alan. Nina seemed to want Alan for a husband, but something was holding her back. Gemma had often sensed it in the long, listening silences that sometimes passed between them during their radio conversations. Nina had not called at all during the last few weeks, making Gemma feel shy about taking the initiative. Something had been wrong for a long time and getting worse, Gemma felt, but she didn't have the courage to question her neighbor.

After a few minutes, she went up to her room, where she lay down and tried to let the tension drain away.

She started to doze, and dreamed of the forest. Eyes looked up at the plateau with curiosity, and she woke up with a start, imagining that somewhere deep in the forest were creatures who were becoming aware of themselves. What would they think if they knew that their world would be taken from them? Nonsense, she told herself. If it was taken from them, they would never know. There would be no one to care because they would never be born.

She sat up, looked out her window, and saw Alan working under the tractor's hood. At least the north field did not have to be planted this year, so he could put in extra time with the harvest army and help his neighbors. He slammed the hood shut and started back toward the house, but three-quarters of the way he turned and went to the family plot and stood there under the trees, head bowed before the stones of their parents and grandparents, and it seemed to her that he was taking an oath.

Suddenly, he looked toward the house, as if he knew she was watching him. Then he started for the fence, and she knew that he was going to walk around the farm, pacing off its limits. He did this once or twice a month, usually before dinner, as if to reaffirm the land's reality. He liked the walk, he said, and the fence had to be checked, but he did it too often, and was hours early today.

She got up and went down into the kitchen, afraid of what he might say to her, doubting herself suddenly, expecting a stranger to come through the door.

3

Gemma kept glancing at Alan throughout dinner, but he avoided her eyes.

Finally, he looked up at her questioningly, his face pale in the harsh electric glare of the naked ceiling bulb. "So there's no chance for you and Cyril?"

She said, "He's not for me."

"And there's no one else? Somebody in town?"

"You know there isn't."

A stern look came into his face, conflicting with his soft brown eyes, which had so often expressed affection for her but were now imprisoned by his growing bitterness. "Well, what do you want?" he asked, but she felt that the question was *What will you ever want?* "I know," he went on before she could answer. "You'd like to run away from everything here if you could. You just don't care about all the effort that's gone into this place." *You don't care for the hard work I'm putting in, or your own,* he was saying, *and you don't care that you're wasting the lives of our parents and grandparents.*

"Try to understand," she said suddenly. "It's because our grandparents lost so much in getting here that we've been unable to better our lives. We need help right now."

He threw up his hands in exasperation. "But the kind of progress you want will only bring disaster."

"That's the excuse for our inability," she answered.

"Oh, no," he shot back. "Human beings were meant to live within narrow limits. What happened on Earth proves that. Give them too much or too little and they lose all sense of direction and values."

"We don't really know what happened on Earth. But we're also facing a disaster here, Alan. To survive we'll have to leave this plateau, but we don't have the means . . . and now there are good reasons why we shouldn't."

Standing up, he said, "I'm going to see Nina. Don't wait up for me."

Gemma started to gather the dishes as he left the kitchen. His bitterness cut into her, and she broke a dish in the sink as he went out the door. She stared at the broken pieces. Maybe he was right. She didn't care, and had finally convinced herself that there was very little to care about.

Two days later, after eating lunch alone, Gemma tuned in the radio for the second meeting between Mayor Overton and the emissary from the mobile. Alan was still at Nina's, since there were no pressing chores to be done before spring planting. Still, he had never been away this long. She wondered if he had decided to marry Nina and bring her home as soon as possible, if only to show his strange sister that he didn't need her and she should get out.

"Well," Mayor Overton said, "what have you come to tell us today?"

"During our last meeting," the offworlder's androgynous voice began, "our exploration teams were already completing their first survey of your planet."

"So you've been here a while," the Mayor said, "long before you contacted us."

"Yes," the offworlder replied.

Sounds of disapproval filled the town hall. "Go on," the Mayor said as they died down.

"We've discovered that one or two forms of animal life may suddenly achieve self-consciousness."

"Suddenly?" the Mayor asked mockingly. "Not in a million years? How convenient for you. Where might they be?"

"I don't think you understand the nature of evolutionary thresholds," the offworlder said. "These creatures have had their million years of preparation, and are ready to step onto the next plateau."

"Are they nearby?"

"You don't need to know that."

"Why?" the Mayor demanded. "Are you afraid that we'll send out armed parties to slaughter them?"

"I would hope that's not what you would do. They should not be disturbed, even by being observed."

"How did you watch them, then?"

"Very discreetly, with special equipment."

"And now you will tell us that this world belongs to these creatures."

"Yes, but we would like to tell each household in your colony personally."

"Personally?" the Mayor asked. "Why? Most of them are hearing what you have to say right now, and those who aren't will get it by word of mouth."

"We have enough volunteers to visit every home," the offworlder said. "They will convey all the facts we have gathered. We believe that personal discussion is best."

"No one will listen to you trying to talk them out of their homes," the Mayor said angrily.

"We will speak only to those who are willing to listen."

"And what will you do after you've spoken to everyone?" the Mayor asked.

"Let people decide for themselves what they wish to do about the problem, if anything."

"And that's all?" the Mayor asked.

"Yes. What else do you imagine we would do?"

"Well, you clearly have the power to enforce your will on us. I don't think many of us, if any at all, will wish to leave our homes for a new life on your mobile."

"Please understand that we never use force, only persuasion. For example, we will offer to show your people the evolving intelligences of this world. Those who make the request to view them will be given the means to judge for themselves."

As Gemma listened to the offworlder's low, clear voice and rational tone, she felt a compelling kinship that went far beyond the issue under discussion. Here was a mind that seemed to have no self-serving preconceptions, that was tolerant yet unafraid to expose hypocrisy, and that would be willing to help any form of intelligent life. Gemma did not feel threatened by the visitor. She wondered, however, what the offworlders would do if their persuasion failed. The emissary had said that they would do nothing at all, but she could not quite understand how that could be. Alan would laugh and say that they didn't really believe what they said, that it was all just talk.

"Go ahead," Mayor Overton said. "Speak to as many people as you wish, for all the good it will do you."

4

Gemma watched the flitter come in low over the newly plowed south field, where Alan usually planted beans. He came out on the porch as the slightly flattened egg-shape settled to the ground on the dirt road that ran past the house.

"They're wasting their time," he said through clenched teeth. "No one's going to get me off the land where my parents are buried." She noticed that he had said *my,* not *our,* parents.

She left him on the porch, went down the steps, and approached the craft, trying to imagine the vast energies that controlled it with such ease, more power than she and Alan could expend in a thousand years of working the farm, and she felt the waste of their lives. Knowledge shaped into a graceful use of power ran the craft, which was probably no more to the people of the mobile than a shovel or scythe was to Alan.

"Well, what are they waiting for?" Alan shouted. "Let's see these superior people."

An oval door opened in the lower half of the vehicle, and a youthful face peered out.

"Greetings!" a young woman's voice called out. "May I approach?"

"Come ahead!" Gemma replied. Alan cleared his throat nervously behind her, and she felt his tension as the visitor stepped out of the craft. She was dressed in brown coveralls and boots.

"My name is Briddy," she said as she came forward.

Gemma looked into a thin, oval, olive-skinned face with dark blue eyes and short black hair. Alan was silent as Gemma turned and led the visitor up the steps.

"My name is Gemma Szigeti, and this is my brother Alan," she said as they all sat down in the wicker chairs. Gemma was about to get up again, but stopped herself. Had the woman been a farmer or townsperson, Gemma would have offered her some food and drink, but she was suddenly unsure. The offworlder might not want to risk contamination with alien microbes. That was foolish, Gemma realized; these people were advanced enough to protect themselves. It was more likely that Briddy would not care for their food; maybe her people regarded food that came from soil or living creatures as disgusting.

Briddy looked at each of them in turn and asked, "You've listened to the radio discussions?"

"Yes," Gemma said.

"I've come to hear your views, and to discuss them with you. And through my link, all my people who have an interest will share in understanding."

"Link?" Alan asked.

Briddy touched her temple. "All of us who wish it may have a link, to whatever degree we wish, to communicate with one another and with the intelligences that care for our lives."

"Intelligences?" Alan asked.

"Minds that grew from simpler designs, and with which we are now engaged in further design, both of them and of ourselves." Alan looked perplexed. "They are our educational, medical, and economic system, supporting our lives," Briddy added. "A second nature, in your view. But let's begin with your views."

Alan gave a nervous laugh. "What? You think that we'll *just* talk and you'll make me see things your way?"

"Either you will or you won't," Briddy replied. "That will be up to you."

"And what about all those others who'll be listening in?" Alan demanded.

"Our discussion will increase their understanding."

"It means nothing at all," Alan said firmly, "your finding a few clever animals in the forest. We're more important than what they may be someday."

Gemma started to feel ashamed of her brother, but was surprised to see that Briddy was listening to him intently, as if he were saying something important.

"Then you'd say," Briddy replied, "that you would have been convinced to leave if we had found fully developed intelligence, but you can't take seriously something still so far ahead in time?"

"Find what you like," Alan said warily. "I won't leave. We'll just have to get along as best we can, that's all."

"But even if you could coexist, let's say successfully," Briddy continued, "would it be fair for you to perturb a natural development that is powerless to resist you? Don't they deserve a chance to develop in their own way?"

"Who?" Alan asked with contempt, making Gemma feel ashamed. "There isn't anyone. All we have is your word that they exist."

"Even if there were no signs of intelligent life on this world," Briddy replied, "the problem would be the same. You would never know what would be lost."

Alan grimaced. "That makes no sense to me."

"Because Earthlike planets will eventually develop intelligent life, sooner or later. And what do you think?" Briddy asked Gemma.

Gemma sighed. "I can't be as certain as my brother."

Briddy sat back in her wicker chair. "Alan, you've said that facts or arguments will never change your mind. That's a curious way to think."

"Now you're going to tell us how to think," Alan said.

Briddy leaned forward. "Thinking's difficult to do correctly. It requires that one strip off all loyalty to group and self-interest, sometimes even to values and traditions, to traditional beliefs and perfectly natural evolutionary impulses, and follow where the observation of facts leads, not where one wishes to go—and the conclusions reached may not be happy ones, however true." She glanced at Gemma. "Most unassisted attempts at thought are little more than a collection of musings and associations."

"My sister will think as I do," Alan said, "when she sees that what you offer would end all that we've made here. It's not worth it."

Briddy smiled. "But equal values sometimes conflict. You were not here first. Does that mean anything to you?"

"How can it, when it means giving up what we've worked for?"

"It would be a great loss, of course, but is there a greater loss to consider?"

"Not from where I sit," Alan said.

Gemma gazed into the offworlder's face, as if she might glimpse something of the woman's life. "Briddy, can you tell us something of the way you live?"

"There may be hundreds of human mobiles in the galaxy by now," Briddy replied. "Each grows in its own way, reproducing as necessary to accommodate population and ways of living, using the vast energies of the cosmos to establish life permanently, in a continuously various culture. These mobiles grew from the few that escaped the death of Earth. But there were other survivors, smaller starships, like the one that brought you here. They settled on planets, with much less success."

"And you disapprove of those," Alan said.

"How old are you, Briddy?" Gemma asked.

"One hundred and three, counting by old Earth years."

Alan grimaced. "You seem happy enough in your ways, so why bother trying to teach us?"

Briddy smiled. "We once imagined that we could free ourselves completely of natural planets. But they are still our visible origins, culturally and biologically. Old Earth survives on perhaps a dozen worlds, in fragmented and backward ways. And because the old song of planets still sings within us, groups of our own people escape to these worlds whenever we enter such a solar system. We let them go, even though their presence will only quicken the destruction of a particular world's native development."

"You let some of your people go?" Alan asked, raising his brows.

Briddy nodded. "For them, life is native to the whole universe, and has a right to spread and compete where it will. I hold the other view, prevalent in most mobiles, that natural planets are the cradles of intelligence, not to be tampered with, and that is why we are interested in what happens here. What you have of Old Earth's culture deserves to develop from strength rather than linger here, scratching the soil for a meager existence, always at risk."

Gemma's interest quickened as she imagined the life of the mobiles. She glanced at her brother and saw that something of the wonder was also catching him up.

"Earthly planets may never be truly habitable," Briddy continued. "Oh, humankind can breathe their atmospheres and drink their waters, but long-term survival inevitably requires extreme measures against native plant and animal life, especially against the microscopic and chemical systems. Human beings can either bioengineer themselves to fit a particular world, or wage decisive war against its life. Native life is either changed or destroyed unfairly if the colony is strong enough to grow. Three of the colonies we've visited have already failed. The rest will sooner or later fail, and we cannot let that happen, as much as it is in our power to prevent it. So we make our offers, to save what we can of what is left of human planetary life, and protect the native life of worlds that is still developing. Your lives could be extended indefinitely and your health secured. You would be given access to broad knowledge, enabling you to grow and change, and become different people over a vast span of time that would be measured in thousands of years, and might one day expand into a large portion of the universe's life. You would have a sense of fulfillment that has for most of human history been felt only in rare moments of inspiration."

Alan got up, trembling. "I can't take any more of this nonsense. You belittle my hard work and tell me that if I stay here I'll either be a failure or some kind of criminal." Gemma looked up at him pleadingly, but he went on. "That's what this person, or whatever it is, is telling us! How can you listen to it?"

"Alan . . ." Gemma started to say as she saw how shocked and hurt he was.

"Go with them and conquer death," he continued. "Live among the pure. But it's not for me. It just can't ever be, because it prevents everything still to come."

"Oh, I see," Briddy said. "You hope for a life after death."

"Our faith tells us that this life shapes us for the next. If you succeed, you go on. If you fail, then you become nothing when you die."

"Success means moral success?" Briddy asked.

"And loyalty to community, steadfastness in hard times. In a word, character that will stand through death."

"And God?" Briddy asked.

"He is unknown, but he will show himself to those who survive life."

"We hope for nothing beyond life," Briddy said, and paused for a moment. "There is no kind way to say it, but all the old religious imaginings, in our view, were a response to the humiliations of living, visions of what intelligence might accomplish in the physical realm, which is spiritual enough. We don't deny the reality of religious feelings, but we know them for what they are, an older way of managing life, of getting people to behave morally."

"And you imagine that you've now got what all the religions promised, in the here-and-now," Alan said with a sneer. "Well, I guess we still need our religion here."

"We've made a good start," Briddy said, "on the road to a greater existence, which we call macrolife."

"But you can't be sure that there isn't another realm," Alan said.

"Perhaps there is, but I don't think so. At the very least we don't support faith by appeals to the unknown. Organized faith, especially, is a self-serving error, a way of forming unimpeachable beliefs as a shield against questioning and the distress of new knowledge. The very nature of codified faith is to resist all argument and proof, all rational longing to learn more, by ending all discussion. Faith forbids all questioning of itself. It is at bottom something familiar—life's natural self-confidence, but this should not be mistaken for knowledge."

Gemma watched as Alan sat down again, looking confused and beaten. "I don't know what you're saying—it sounds insanely arrogant to me. Get out of here! We'll survive whether you help us or not."

"What you fear," Briddy said, "is that in our control of death we cling to this side of the horizon, denying ourselves what you call further spiritual growth. But you should not fear this, because we do grow and learn."

Alan glared at her, then looked away. The visitor from the stars rose to leave.

"Briddy!" Gemma said suddenly. "Show me what you found in the forest. I want to see for myself." She looked at her brother, but he refused to meet her eyes. "I have to, Alan. There's no other way to be sure. Try to understand, and come with me."

He stared down at his feet, unable to answer.

"You're among the first to make this request," Briddy said. "I will arrange it." She left the porch and walked toward her flitter. Alan was silent as the craft lifted from the ground, but his face was taut with tension.

Gemma knelt by her brother and tried to embrace him.

"Alan, please! We'll be losing nothing by seeing for ourselves. Just think, if all this is true, then there's nothing we can ever lose. We'll have everything."

He looked at her for a moment, and shook his head in denial. "You're losing yourself," he muttered.

5

Alan ignored her all during the next day, going about his chores with a silence that accused her of betrayal.

"It's not wrong for me to try to find out all I can," she said at dinner. The kitchen window was open, letting in an unusually warm breeze from the south, bringing the spicy smells of the forest.

"And what will that be?" he asked.

"Whatever there is."

"Whatever they want you to see. You'll end up thinking as they do, because that's what they're set to do here, make us believe what they think."

Hurt, she asked, "Do you really believe I'm a child that can be led around by the nose?"

"You always could talk."

"That's not fair, Alan."

"What's fair got to do with it? Doing right may not be pleasant." He laughed. "Even that Briddy agrees with that!"

"You're twisting things, Alan, ignoring what's really going on. The entire colony has looked the other way for three generations."

"We've been busy surviving."

"If only you'd take the trouble to think."

"I have thought about it. I listened to . . . that person, or whatever it is, spout nonsense for over an hour, and all I could see was how it was working on you, making you into someone else."

"Is that all you saw?" Gemma asked, searching his face until he glared back at her.

That night Gemma dreamed of creatures from the forest climbing up to the plateau and peering through her window. The round eyes looked deeply into her. She gazed back and saw self-awareness increasing toward the day when it would look up at the stars through a clear midnight, and question. A thousand years hence, a hundred thousand, a million? Was that too long to matter?

And then the eyes became her brother's, but still set in an alien face, and she woke up. The warm breeze was still wafting in from the forest through the open window of her bedroom, whispering about growing things—molds, mushrooms and rotting wood, and flowers.

She lay back and tried to sleep, and in a moment the eyes were at her window again.

It was afternoon, two days later, when the flitter landed again in front of the house. Gemma hurried out to the craft, not wanting to provoke Alan, and slipped quickly inside as the lock opened.

There were two people in the cabin with Briddy. Gemma was startled to see that one of them was Nina, and that the other was Cyril's stepbrother Nathaniel. She nodded at them in greeting.

"I take it you three know each other?" Briddy asked.

"Yes," Gemma said, wondering whether Alan had known about Nina's plans, and if they had disagreed about it. If he knew he was going to lose Nina, then that would explain some of his anger and confusion.

It was very quiet in the cabin. Gemma sat down next to Briddy and waited. Nina and Nathaniel smiled at her shyly and seemed reluctant to speak. She noticed that the tall, thin Nathaniel was sitting very close to his stocky stepsister. A screen lit up in the padded, egg-shaped cabin. Gemma saw Alan on the porch, looking up anxiously at the departing craft, and the sight of her brother's shrinking image saddened her.

The only sense she had of motion came from the landscape of farms and small houses unrolling on the screen. The flat roofs and straight dirt roads of the town rushed into view for an instant, and then the craft sailed over the edge of the plateau and out over the forest.

Gemma looked back to Nina and Nathaniel, and suddenly understood what they meant to each other. "I see," she murmured. "I should have guessed it after all the times we've talked."

"It's true," Nina said, her hand slipping into Nathaniel's. He held it awkwardly. "We've been lovers for a long time." She smiled. "We had to keep it a secret. But no one can forbid it now."

So that was why Cyril and Nathaniel did not get along, Gemma realized. Cyril must have discovered his sister's secret love for their stepbrother. It occurred to her that Nina and Nathaniel might not really care about what the offworlders had come to tell the colony, but only saw the mobile as a way of escape to a place where they could be together. Or perhaps they understood the greater life they had been offered and wanted to leave. Things were getting tangled in ways she had not expected. It seemed possible that Nina had even used Alan to hide her life with Nathaniel. Could Alan have known all this time? That would explain why he had not been rushing to marry Nina.

"I'm sorry," Nina said softly, "if this is a shock to you."

"It's the only way for us now," Nathaniel added, "for better or worse. I understood that after I attended the meetings."

"What do Cyril . . . and Alan think?" Gemma asked.

"Alan tried to understand for a long time," Nina said sadly. "He thought I might get over it. Cyril . . ."

"He blackmailed us," Nathaniel said angrily, "to please himself. He knew what people in town would think if they found out, how hard it would be for either of us to go there if anyone found out. He knew that Alan would have been shamed in public by the truth. We'll be free of both of them forever."

As Gemma looked into Nina's and Nathaniel's anxious eyes, she realized that they had been prisoners, and deserved a better life. She reached over and grasped their hands for a moment. Tears came into Nina's eyes. Nathaniel seemed moved, but held his feelings in check.

"Thank you," Nina managed to say, "for understanding. Alan tried for so long, but it was impossible."

Poor Alan, Gemma thought, he'll be abandoned by everyone who had been close to him.

Briddy had been gazing at the screen almost too intently, as if sensing that Gemma and her neighbors needed privacy. Now she turned toward them and said, "We're on an automatic tour." The flitter dropped low and raced over the forest canopy. "We've got small drones in the area that will send what they see to our screen. There!"

Gemma caught a flash of silver among the greenery as the image on the screen changed with flashing speed. "We're seeing through the drone's eyes now," Briddy continued.

As the picture slowed down, Gemma peered down into the forest and saw that the drone was following a well-worn path of red clay through the green and black shadows. Suddenly it caught up with two creatures moving down the trail on all fours.

"They're headed for water," Briddy said as the image steadied. Gemma saw large hairy heads set on heavy torsos pushing forward with long hind legs that reminded her of grassy stalks. The creatures entered a patch of sunlight, stopped and raised their forelegs from the ground. The drone moved around in front of them and Gemma found herself looking directly into large white eyes.

"They take the drone for some kind of insect," Briddy said as both pairs of eyes stared into the screen and Gemma imagined a future civilization of clothed beings who still exhibited the expressions of these creatures, speaking a strange language, seeing the universe in odd ways, longing for things she could not even guess at.

After a few moments the creatures lost interest in the drone and began to scratch at the bark of a nearby tree. Nothing much to see, her brother would have said, just an animal that sometimes goes on two legs. We're no danger to them up here.

"We've examined dead ones," Briddy said, "and it's all there in the brain and physiology, the next step. It will happen."

"Can you be certain?" Gemma asked, hearing her brother's voice in the question.

"As certain as seeing a solar system form in the clouds of a new sun."

"Have you seen that happen?" Gemma asked, remembering the old astronomy books she had displayed on a reader that had finally failed.

Briddy nodded. "And I've watched a sun die."

"There they go," Nathaniel said.

The creatures were off again down the trail. The drone fell back, followed at a distance, and broke through the trees to catch sight of the creatures bathing in a small lake with several dozen of their kind.

"Listen," Briddy whispered.

Laughter-like singing mingled with the sound of splashing as the bipeds played in the sun-shot water.

6

"Is that all you're taking with you?" Alan asked as Gemma finished packing her canvas bag.

She looked around her room quickly. "I'll have everything I need there," she said.

Alan sat down on the edge of the bed. "You're sure?" he asked, as if hoping to hold her back with the question.

She nodded, avoiding his eyes, knowing that they would plead with her even if he said nothing.

"I guess there was never much here that you wanted," he said, which was an improvement over saying that she would take any excuse to leave a life of hard work.

She looked at him finally, and saw the resignation in his eyes; no pleading self-pity, just resignation. "I'm going," she said, "because I can't live here knowing what will happen. It's the right thing to do, even if I were the only one."

"But it's useless," he said. "Most are staying. You won't change anything."

"There are other ways to live," she answered. "I can do the right thing, for myself, and as an example, no matter how useless."

"What do you really think of the people who are coming here?" In his mind it counted against her.

"Briddy told me that it happens," she said. "Every time a mobile enters a sunspace, there are those among them who are drawn to planets. It's best when there's a colony they can join, where they might be needed. If there isn't, they're often never heard from again."

"You'll have to learn a whole new life."

"The mobile always needs new people to increase its biological diversity. You'll benefit in the same way from those who are coming here. I'll learn. It should be interesting." She paused, wondering if she sounded almost too much like Briddy. "I'm sorry about you and Nina."

"I'll find someone else." He was silent for a moment. "They wanted to convince us, but they wouldn't do anything about it when we refused to leave. I didn't expect that." He sounded relieved. "It must not mean that much to them."

"What did you expect? That they would force us all to leave? They did all they could." She sat down on the edge of her bed for the last time. "Don't you understand even now?"

"We'll do the best we can, about the creatures," he said softly, "at least in my lifetime. Strange, to think you'll be alive long after I'm gone. We'll never see each other again."

"I'm sorry," she said, surprised by the coldness in her voice, even though she knew he was trying to reach out to her as much as he could, in his own way.

"You really do think we're living in the past here, don't you?" he asked.

"Yes," she said, again coldly, "and I can't be part of it," and her resolve wavered for a moment as she tried to summon her reasons for leaving, some of them vague and impulsive, others clear and impossible to ignore. She thought of the thousands of jars of preserves she had set up over the years, the countless meals she had cooked, the thousands of books she could not have but had seen references to in the meager data storage of the surviving readers, and the frustrated hunger for knowledge that had grown within her until it could swallow the universe. The hope of knowledge was like new air in her lungs, enabling her to breathe freely for the first time in her life. She would spend the next twenty-five years learning where she had come from and who she might become.

"I would go with you," he said almost calmly, "but I just can't after all the work I've put into this place."

"I know," she answered, trying to sound kind as she thought that it was his stubborn pride that made him feel he had to stay. "You imagine the dead judging you as if they were alive," she continued. "That's living in the past that's dead and gone, and neither of us ever knew what it was. Why not accept that this place gave us a refuge for a time, but that now we have to move on?"

She looked out the window. The flitter was a dark shadow sliding down the white fabric of the curtains sewn by her grandmother.

"You do look down on us," Alan said bitterly, his voice breaking.

"Read some history, Alan. Learn what the books have tried to remember for us—what we did to Old Earth."

"I know all that," he said.

"But you think it means you have to live the way you do so it won't happen again. But it will, if you go on like this. I know that the mobiles don't make deserts around themselves, which is what our kind will make of this planet, of any planet, once we get off on the wrong foot." She spoke without looking at him, hoping that at any moment he would say that he was coming with her.

"I had no idea . . . that you'd thought about this so much," he said, standing before her, his shoulders sagging.

She got up, embraced him, and held his head against her shoulder. "Come with me," she said with a shudder, determined that her words would seize his will and change it.

He sighed and pushed her away. "I just can't. You may be right, but I can't simply force myself to see it." He looked into her eyes. "Can you understand that?"

She nodded, holding her feelings in check. "Maybe someday we'll be back this way. Alan, you don't know what it was like to look into the eyes of the creatures who may be the real people of this world. They'll have enough to overcome without having to deal with us. They deserve to have their world to themselves."

He gave her a defeated look, and she was unable to accept that he would be long dead when her life was still beginning.

"Alan," she said, resolved to try again, "you'll die here. Come with me and live, even if you don't understand, even if you can't feel it's right. One day you will understand."

He was silent, then said with a bitter smile, "I'll return to nature."

"To what?" she asked. "To the nature we transplanted here from jars after we burned the plateau?"

"It's all nature—everywhere," he said in a breaking voice.

"We had no right," she replied helplessly.

"We took only as much as we needed to live. It was live or die, coming here. I have to go on."

When he was silent she looked toward her shabby bag and decided that she wouldn't take anything with her, then went out through the open door of her room for the last time, through the short hall and out the front door, pausing on the porch steps that she had once watched her father and Alan rebuild, noticing that the job would soon have to be done again. The paving stones Alan had set in the path from the house were unchanged, she saw as she went down the steps and hurried across to the dirt road.

The flitter's lock opened for her, and she stepped inside, refusing to look back.

Nina and Nathaniel were waiting in the flitter's cabin, looking uncertain as Gemma sat down across from them. She realized that they had feared she might decide not to come at the last moment; her arrival seemed to reassure them.

"How many others?" Gemma asked as the flitter lifted and her world fell away on the screen.

"Fifty-one," Briddy said. "Perhaps another time we'll do better, if we come this way again and the colony is still here." For the first time, Gemma sensed a touch of sadness in Briddy's voice. "Perhaps if Earth had not destroyed itself, there would not have been this desperate colonization of planets."

"How many colonies are there?" Nina asked.

"Nine out of twelve are left," Briddy replied, "within a hundred-light-year radius of Earth. If Earth had lived, mobile habitats would have proliferated routinely in its sunspace, and sooner or later some of them would have set out for the stars, reproducing themselves independently of natural worlds, leaving planets alone, for better or worse, as the nurseries of intelligent life. We let some of our people return to the cradle, if only to prevent the death of these colonies, and because we have not changed ourselves sufficiently to forget this yearning for the daylight of worlds." She paused and looked at them more intently before going on. "We accept that there is no perfect way for intelligence to arise and flourish. Our macrolife removes us from the unconscious game of nature's worlds, but we still carry that nature in our bodies even as we strive to change ourselves and break the constraints—no, the tyranny of space-time. If that seems contradictory to you, let me point out that the native possibilities of this planet may also fail. We try to leave as many ways open as possible."

"Do you believe the colony will fail?"

"Given the biological diversity we've just given it, it may live for a while. Will it be enough? Probably not. A hundred individuals, more or less, may not make a difference. But we may return here in a century, and then everyone may wish to join us."

Gemma felt overwhelmed by complexities, but confirmed in her decision. It was not what she had expected. Although the mobile was leaving behind some people—malcontents, Alan had called them—they were not permitted to bring any major technologies with them, only their personal skills. The colony would not benefit as she had imagined. The problem was not resolved, except for her and a few others—thinking only of themselves, Alan had said.

But she could not have stayed, waiting for the colony to expand from the plateau, preventing the forest creatures from starting their climb toward the light. Even if the human population behaved like saints, subtle changes in the planet's ecology would begin to spread as soon as the colony outgrew the plateau.

Suddenly she felt that nothing would be as she had imagined, that an alien life waited for her, and that home was in the folds of the planetary crust behind her. . . .

But the doubting moment passed as she looked at the

screen and saw the world where she had been born grow small. The view flashed to the mobile, and she saw a giant egg-shape swimming in the starry night, waiting to receive her.

Far Futures

Transfigured Night

". . . pass beyond the service economy, beyond the imagination of today's economists; we shall become the first culture in history to employ high technology to manufacture that most transient yet lasting of products: the human experience.

". . . blurring of the line between the real and the unreal will confront the society with serious problems, but it will not prevent or even slow the emergence of the psyche-service industries and psychocorps.

". . . sequences of experience so organized that their very juxtaposition with one another will contribute color, harmony or contrast to lives that lack these qualities . . . frameworks for those whose lives are otherwise too chaotic and unstructured."

—Alvin Toffler, *Future Shock*

"I begin with two possibilities which are quite probably realized, though not by normal men; namely, that Smith remembers that twenty years ago he was Jones and also Robinson, while Macgregor and Stuart each remember that twenty years ago they were Johnston . . .

"If we divide a flatworm in two, both halves may live happily ever after. If each gets a fair share of the nervous system, presumably they get a certain amount of memory from their common parent. And the converse holds when two protozoa fuse. The case of disassociated personality in men is hardly apposite, as two different personalities rarely if ever seem to be fully conscious at the same time. Human consciousnesses do not usually split or unite in this way because human bodies do not. If, on the other hand, as is widely supposed, consciousness may continue without a body, I see no reason why such restrictions should hold. But I leave it as a problem for a person sincerely desirous of immortality whether he would prefer that 100 years hence fifteen distinct spirits each remembered having been he, or that one spirit remembered being he and also fourteen other people. For clearly if 100 years hence someone remembers having been I, I have not died, even though he is less like me than I am now like myself at four years old."

—J. B. S. Haldane, *Possible Worlds*

"The chief implications [of indefinitely extended life] concern the sanity and outlook of the individual . . ."

—R. C. W. Ettinger, *Man Into Superman*

1 / Quantum Mutata

Eternals! I hear your call gladly.
Dictate swift winged words & fear not
To unfold your dark visions of torment.

—William Blake

Thrushcross watched the birth of his father.

As the unclad body was borne upward out of the long-term nutrient bath, Thrushcross selected fitting responses from his repertoire of sensitivities. His face softened into attentive radiance; feelings of joyous love blossomed within him, moistening his eyes, settling him into a blissful acceptance of the event.

The moments of caring passed slowly. His thoughts followed a prayer of understanding. It entered his mind as he watched the crystalline liquid fall from the suspended body. *Death once gave renewal. We die by degrees, discarding memories, keeping what we please of ourselves. We renew our bodies without the sacrifice of death. We shape ourselves. We go on despite forgetfulness . . .*

The frame was never to be forgotten. To receive its meanings was the only prayer permitted by the circling illuminati, who maintained the frame of Earth.

Thrushcross's feelings developed. He knelt down trembling before the raised form (to meditate further would result in the recording of special graces); pride, triumph, and delight filled his being.

These sensations had persisted in unconscious forms through the ages before the beginning of the game periods more than five thousand years ago. All life moments within the frame's container were the work of planners and their descendants, the illuminati; their choices were his own.

The pulse of his life was his own creation from one moment to the next, unlike the crude, unchosen flow of experience known by the unchanged. The unchanged men, he thought, are such frail creatures—clinging to every powerless instant before melting back into nature, where death is the only way of summoning up new individuals.

Emerging from renewal, his father would live his next sequence as desperately as the unchanged still lived their struggle for mere survival.

The last words of the prayer entered him. *Free actions and formless things shaping themselves into intense contrasts and varieties: a goal worthier than all others . . .*

All this the planners had taught.

Droplets of remaining liquid glistened on his father's body. The skin was smooth and hairless. The flesh was new; the brain and nervous system were new, yet retaining the vital past.

Thrushcross stood up behind the clear partition, anxious now to rejoin his own life. In the flow of time he would often impinge upon the sequence of a relative or known person. At times he would be older than his parents; at other times he would not know them. To intersect with recognition was rare. Thrushcross stood motionless as his father's eyes opened to look at him across the centuries . . .

It was only half a recognition; the youthful green eyes did not know him. Thrushcross wondered suddenly why he had come to his father's reanimation.

In the private time of his own sequence, Thrushcross sought colors in the void. His will reached into the cube's black field and folded out a visible pattern from the spatial infrastructure.

A triangle of light.

The points glowed into stars.

Yellow. Orange. Red.

He relaxed his concentration and the field went blank. Why was it taking so long for the sequence to quicken? A pale shimmer of light marked his unease. His sudden lack of interest turned the cube's inside a hopeless black, a space larger than everything outside it.

He looked around at the bare studio, got up, and went up the flight of stairs leading out into the alcove in the north corner of his living room.

Beams of light, focused by the giant lens of the picture

window, crossed the green carpet. It was spring outside. Thrushcross stepped out of the alcove and walked through the streaming light into the center of the room. A soft wind fluttered the short grass in front of the house. The black road was a chasm running through the tall oaks, a section of night where no one traveled.

Thrushcross thought of the estates beyond the roadway, dwellings for two million persons around the world; behind each person lay the memories of countless lifetimes. How often had he lived through the stored sequences of others? Somewhere someone was now living one of his own forgotten lifetimes. Among the unchanged someone had died; another would certainly die tomorrow; and one would be born, to grow into self-awareness for the first time, with no promise of a past. He thought of Evelyn in her house down the road. She was waiting for him.

Thrushcross stood perfectly still, waiting for the sequence to quicken.

Slowly, the substance of darkness spilled out of the roadway and ate the spring day. Stars pierced the night.

He went up close to the picture window and peered outside. A wind rustled the tree near the house. By the light streaming out from the living room, he saw the leaves change color as the night wind turned them over; they relaxed, turned, fluttering like fingers plucking invisible harpstrings . . .

He turned back to the brightness of the living room. A vague fear constricted his chest, and he took a deep breath.

The lights went out. He looked around at the dark shapes of motionless furniture transformed suddenly into crouching beasts. The picture window was a cave mouth with a howling wind outside. The dull gong of the doorbell seemed to float up from his bowels.

He walked to the front entrance, turned the brass knob, and opened the door. No one.

But as he looked up, he thought he saw a black, shoulder-like silhouette obscuring the stars. The ground trembled slightly and he gripped the door frame with both hands. The warm wind quickened its soughing through the oaks. A great figure of some kind had bent down to the house to ring the doorbell.

Thrushcross closed the door and went back into the living room. The lights slowly dimmed and flickered.

He looked around the living room, noticing how dusty it seemed to have become, as if years had passed in the few moments he had taken to check the front door.

He went to the picture window and saw that the eastern sky was filling with orange light and great low-lying cumulus clouds. Beams of light stabbed down onto the roadway.

He stepped back and sat down in the high-backed chair that faced the window. Feelings of concern for Evelyn stormed into him as he summoned the sight of his father's eyes. Inertia imprisoned him in the chair as a desire to visit Evelyn seized him.

The orange light grew brighter, passing through the window like a threatening tide. He got up and forced himself to walk to the door. Opening the door seemed a slow process. He stepped outside.

The clouds drove quickly from the lighted east, staining the night sky. He turned around and saw the house lights blinking through the open doorway, as if a fire were raging inside.

Memories flickered just beyond recognition.

Urgently he turned from the house and ran down to

the road. From there he looked back at the assembly of interconnected domes, in reality, globes set in the Earth; the windows flickered with white light, and the picture window suggested the eye of a giant. At any moment Central would activate the buried colossus and he would tear his way out of the ground, scattering dirt and rock around himself.

Thrushcross felt his body readying itself, preparing him for the dangers of the sequence. He walked into the center of the road and started to run toward Evelyn's house. He slowed suddenly and continued in a fast walk, puzzled by the involuntary reversal.

He felt apprehensive as he walked. The road curved right and he saw the house, three interconnected pyramids with flattened apexes and triangular windows. The lights were blinking inside.

The wind was growing stronger; the clouds were darkening, creating enclaves in the orange expanse. There was a smell of flowers on the wind. Despite the rush of air in his ears, Thrushcross felt the stillness inside the house as he came up to the open front door.

He went inside, turned right, and entered the oval living room. Looking up through the skylight, he saw the ghastly heavens pressing down on the house. The orange light fell into the room like a fog, discoloring the red rug.

Her body lay in the center of the room, headless.

Thrushcross slowly became aware of a man standing in the far right corner of the room. He held Evelyn's head by the hair. In the flickering light, Thrushcross saw that the intruder wore long black hair to the waist; his features were coarse, thick lips open in a sneer.

Catlike, the figure rushed him, knocking him down as it went past into the hall and out the front door. Fixed in

Thrushcross's mind was Evelyn's face, eyes shut in sorrow, long red hair drawn tightly by the weight of the head. As he got up, Thrushcross could not decide which to do first—go after the head or attend to the body.

He ran outside, down to the road, and continued into the lighted east. The wind pressed him back, thickening the air into a barrier which struck him in the chest and face. Ahead of him, his mother's head was a black ball swinging back and forth in the running shadow's hand.

2 / Line of Darkness

> "I believe the moment is near when by a procedure of active paranoiac thought, it will be possible to systemize confusion and contribute to the total discrediting of the world of reality."
>
> —SALVADOR DALI

The orange brilliance of the east was becoming a bright yellow. Thrushcross could no longer see the fleeing marauder. He slowed to a walk. His heart beat steadily, an acoustical sun at the center of his universe, sounding loudly over the rush of air in his ears.

The yellow glare swept toward him, dissolving all sight of road and horizon. Thrushcross stopped, turned around once, and lost all sense of direction. Dust rose from the ground around him.

He felt frustration and anger. Images of mutilation played in his brain. He pulled the arms and legs from the intruder's body; he dug the eyes out of the head; ripped the tongue from its mouth; shattered the teeth with a stone. The mouth filled with blood, becoming a deep pool of thickening liquid.

He ran, legs working furiously, but they did not carry

him out from the realm of yellow light. He tried another direction, and another, with no result.

He stopped and was still. He breathed, he saw, he heard the sound of his heart; but who was he? There was something he had to do—

—the moment of discontinuity passed. The light cleared and he saw a red plain ahead, dunes to his left and right. Overhead the sun was too bright to look at, a smear of white heat in a deep blue sky. A warm, dry blast of sand hit him; as he turned away he glanced back in the direction from which he had come—

—blackness where the cadmium sands ended, a wall of darkness at the edge of the world, as tall as the sky, right and left into the vanishing point. Its blackness seemed to be absorbing daylight, as if reality had been cut open here to reveal the night beyond.

He ran up a high dune to his left and looked away from the barrier. Heat waves rippled the image of a plateau. The view jiggled into clarity and he saw white cliffs.

Squinting, he noticed that something spiderlike was climbing up a portion of cliff face. The heat magnified and distorted the limbs, making them even more insectlike.

The fleeing figure reached the top and disappeared over the edge of the tableland. As he watched, Thrushcross noticed the faint images of two cloud-wrapped peaks standing far back on the plateau.

He turned again to the black wall. Its surface changed into a front of billowing storm clouds filled with silent lightning. He thought he heard an ocean, the crying of sea birds, beached fish flapping on the packed wet sand until the waves rushed in again to pull them out—

—and the clouds pulled themselves over the desert like a blanket of steel wool unrolling to the sound of grinding gears. Rain fell slowly, sorrowfully, with the rhythm of a rhyming verse.

The desert melted into brown mud. The sky was an inverted black floor pierced with small holes; right side up it would have been a fountain instead of a drain.

A yellow glow was trying to break out from behind the peaks on the plateau. The rain ran down the cliffs, staining them dark gray.

Thrushcross looked up into the raindrops, expecting that at any moment he would fall into the sky, to the surface below; but the setting remained the same, refusing to flip over according to his anticipation. *Good, Good,* he thought as the water washed his face. He waited.

The rain stopped, leaving small rivulets running away into the sand. A great creature had been slaughtered beyond the sky, and the desert was soaking up the fallen blood, reddening itself further. Heat mists rose from the sands, vapors swirling around Thrushcross, closing up space until he could not see five feet in any direction. He sat down on the wet sand and waited for the universe to open up again.

A crablike creature crawled out of the mists, a moving death's head leading with a single claw. Thrushcross looked at it carefully as it jerked slowly forward on the loose sand, past him and back into the fog.

He stood up and saw that the mists now extended only as high as his waist. A giant, he had poked his head through the clouds and wondered why he could see only snow fields. The shallow mists floated gently over the sands, secure and lazy, as if waiting for the world to change beneath their cover.

Far away the cliffs floated on the whiteness. Beneath a

bleached sky the twin peaks imprisoned an orange fire in their valley. Thrushcross thought of Evelyn's head, consciousness scattered from behind its eyes, sparks wandering now in a starless waste of the unclaimed. *I remember, I remember,* he thought as he began to run slowly toward the plateau. Halfway there he quickened his pace; his eyes searched for a way up as he came close.

He saw a series of handholds cut into the white chalk wall. Inhaling white dust, he climbed, feeling the softness in his palms and fingers.

As he reached the edge and looked over across the tableland, a strange quiet drifted into him. Tall grass moved in a slow breeze. The two peaks dominated, casting sharply cut shadows across the grainlike plain of grass.

Thrushcross stepped over the edge with one knee, then the other. He stood up slowly, at peace. A permanence hung over the land, as if thoughts were draining out of the world, to come back, in time, as new physical objects for his appreciation.

As he began his walk to the mountains, he pictured a vast hollow area inside the plateau, a region of resonances, where thoughts and wishes aspired to musical utterance, where the dreams of all who lived within the frame of Earth were channeled into a mighty river running out of chaos into the reality of, for him, a green plain, unbroken blue sky, mountains, and the lure of what lay beyond. *I remember, I remember,* he thought again as he hurried.

Beyond the jungle of the valley ahead of him, the horizon was a blinding wall of light, its upward glow suffusing the blue sky. The rocky barrens of the mountain pass were behind him. Ahead, the Earth sloped downward into the tangled greenery.

The smell of corruption reached him on a sudden gust of wind, the whisper of a desperate messenger. The way became steeper, and he saw the swamp.

Here the forest's knotty roots were met in vast networks of crotches, elbows, and open-fingered hands. Mist rose into the mass of leaf and vine overhead, but some of the glow from outside still filtered through, bathing the swamp in a bleak yellow. The vegetation seemed to breathe with an endless sadness, concealing a pathos which mocked profundity. The thought surprised and puzzled Thrushcross.

He came to the water's edge, stopped for a moment, and tried to remember, then continued to his right along the sandy shore. A hundred feet ahead stood a tree, its drooping branches dipping into the stagnant water, weary limbs straining to lie down upon their own reflection.

Thrushcross walked closer and saw Evelyn's head hanging on a branch like a rotting fruit. Her mouth was an open *o,* eyes closed to shut out the stroke of her attacker's blade.

Thrushcross summoned a shudder; his body shook and he tasted sweat on his upper lip. *Good,* he thought. He searched for the intensity of fear, and found it coiled snakelike in his stomach.

Suddenly a spear of light left his mother's mouth and lanced out across the green water, a hundred yards across the oily stillness, to a small encrusted island, to touch a shining slender metal shaft standing there on spidery undergear, pointing like a cathedral spire to the sickly yellow sky.

Thrushcross saw a dark figure step out from behind the tree. Evelyn's murderer raised a spear and hurled it—

—directly into Thrushcross's solar plexus. The jolt of penetration threw him back; his arms flew out as the message of pain traced out the complex circuit of his nervous system. His hands closed around the lance and pulled it out. The attacker drew a machete and reached Thrushcross in two leaps, swinging the blade in a whistling arc that caught him in the neck, throwing his head upward—

—he saw his trunk fall with hands still clutching the spear, felt the blood rush up after his head, pulse out from his heart. It took forever for the head to fall; he was suspended within an instant of time, buoyed up by the force of his denial. He tried to shout, but his sound shot out as a cord of light touched the spire point on the islet, and faded.

Below him, the blood from his body soaked into the sand.

He lay in a dream-filled night. The pain in his open neck vessels reached out after his severed head to lure it back. He felt no pain in his head. Liberated, it floated in the starry darkness, jealous of its freedom, wondering how it could ever have been part of the broken thing lying on the pallid sands below. *An accident in the game sequence, was it possible?*

The past came into his brain, comforting him with its age—

—his body agonized, welling blood—

—memories fell like stones into the mirror surface of an azure pool, creating circles of wave fronts drifting into the past—

—he was looking down into a valley of dying stars, glowing coals left over from the fire of a devouring creation. Time reversed itself and the stars flared up as if a sudden wind had breathed upon them—

—he stood in a hot wind under a desert sun. The speed at which life passes slowed, and he was speaking to his warriors in the dusty square of the village. ". . . we must hew our days," he was saying, "as if from stone. We are better for this than those who have changed their bodies and spirits, who leave the Earth for an outer darkness, which is also within them . . ."—

—what a savage I was in those endless days of my first century, living among the unchanged. I was one of them—Herdal, who lived long enough to fall in love with an outsider—

—"I've been awake all the nights of this year," Rydpat said to the cocked ear of his diary, "hoping for peace, for some kind of contentment, no matter how small, before dawn comes. Day is turmoil, unfocused, uncontemplative, a scattered light. Night is space to think in . . ." He stopped and listened as his mind-linked harpsichord dusted the space of his house with tinkling notes. Each series was the direct analogue of preceding thoughts, which had to be clearly stated and elegant. "Only my most painful memories create the best sounds . . ."—

—To what purpose are these selves retrieved? Who is forcing me to see them again? The unchanged Herdal, Rydpat the composer, and others had long ago passed from his self during renewals. It was not part of sequences to look back so overtly.

—Who are you? he thought, wondering why the illuminati were failing to protect him. Was the intruder more powerful?

There were no answers to his questions. Alone he was powerless to bear himself out of the transfixed state. Plucked one by one, he knew, from the stores of the illuminati, memories began to exist once more, living things, invasions sharper than any spear point, fears of origin, kindly murdered long ago . . . crying to be restated, examined, redeemed, understood, accepted. . . .

2-1 / The Unchanged

> ". . . any sweeping change in man is likely to become worldwide; there will be no reservoir of unchanged men to follow alternate possibilities, unless we consciously choose to maintain such a reservoir."
>
> —GERALD FEINBERG, *The Prometheus Project: Mankind's Search for Long-Range Goals*

Herbal lay under the desert stars, shivering in his blanket. A fire would only reveal him to whoever had been tracking him for the last two days.

At his right towered The Eye's Bright Treasure, snowy peaks with rock like blue metal, lower reaches draped in shadows. In those shadows lay the cave of those who had gone before, all now lost forever. To reach the cave was a difficult journey across swamp, desert, stone-sharp foothills, glacier—a test of his right to lead. One day in years ahead he would fail to come back, and the one who came after him would arrange the bones on his first visit, mingling them with all the others in the great pit at the back of the cave deep within the mountain.

Did they think him so weak that they would send the next one so soon? He had led his people for only six years. It had to be a stranger, maybe from outside, from the dreamlife that had taken his mother long ago. . . .

Herdal turned away from the mountains, pressed his cheek to the cooling sand flat, and watched the dark line of horizon. The sky was deep blue in the bright starlight; it would be easy to see the silhouette of anything moving toward him.

A bump appeared at the edge of the world, the black

center of an unseen spider, growing larger as it crept toward him; it stopped.

He watched for a long time, as he had for the last two nights; the pursuer was motionless, asleep. Slowly Herdal closed his eyes and rolled on his back—

Eyes followed him as he left the village. Toothless women sat in front of their adobe houses. Children stopped to watch him as he walked through their playing. The men were in the swamp forest, hunting small game, snakes and fishes. The younger women were planting grain in the field. The oldest men were asleep.

He saw his father's eyes inside himself. All his life Rastaban had gone to the invisible wall, to gather the food which appeared daily. Those who followed the way of honor hated him and those like him. Herdal hated him also, but gave his protection. The old man ate the leavings of the powerful ones who had taken his wife; he had traded his young son's mother for a lifetime of eating without effort. Herdal walked the way of honor for himself and for his father; and the village knew that for this reason Herdal would always come back from the cave, even when he became old. For his father's faults Herdal would not die in the cave; his bones would belong to the desert. There would be no one to take them to the cave, even if they were found.

—bright lights blinded him, brighter than the sun, yet it was too early for sunrise. He threw off his blanket, jumped up and shouted at his pursuer, "Come and face me, coward! What trick is this!"

Something fell over him and he began to claw his way through it, straining to break the strands. He struggled, but the net was pulled tighter and he fell. The lights went off and he lay still in the dawnlight.

A figure came and knelt down over him, touching his

thighs, tearing open a few of the leather stitches that held the pieces of his pants together. Hands reached in to check his genitals, then pulled at the hair on his chest. He heard a laugh, like a boy's giggle.

A sliver of sun pushed up over the horizon, spilling light across the barren flat. Herdal looked up and saw a tall woman standing over him, her face pale under a dark, wide-rimmed hat. The rest of her was covered in unbroken silver. She was thin and bony, her hips protruding grotesquely. An outsider for sure, he thought. Behind her stood a three-wheeled vehicle, its twin lamps still bright in the daylight.

"You smell horribly," she said in his own words, "but we'll clean you up and you'll do fine." She knelt down to him again. "Were you going to that awful cave with all the bones?"

He nodded, and poked his right hand through the net to grab her face. She fell back on her heels and kicked him. "You'll like it better after some changes." Her nostrils flared and he wondered if she really had two hearts and had lived more than one lifetime.

She looked at him intently, then reached forward and seized his left wrist with a grasp of iron. "I'll let you out if you behave."

He nodded again. She took out a pair of metal jaws and began cutting the net. "You're really magnificent, you know."

When he was free and standing, he saw that she was a head taller than he, and larger in chest and shoulders despite her bony frame. He watched her as she went back to her three-wheeler. She turned off the lights, took out a small package from behind the seat, came back, and dropped it at his feet. "Take off those rotting things and put these on."

"No," he said.

"Why not?"

"My parents and friends made what I have to last a long time—"

"That won't be long from the way it looks."

"—and it would show I have little respect for the labor of my people."

"I can't wait that long," she shouted. "Put these on!" She came up close, grabbed his shirt, and ripped it off with one motion, burning him with the leather; then she grasped the waist of his pants and pulled, tearing the seam as he was thrown to the ground.

He lay on his back, humiliated. She was strong, and unafraid to use her strength. It would be best to do as she wanted, until a better moment; he would use her garments until he could repair his own. He sat up, pulled the bundle to himself, and began unfolding it. Standing up, he looked away from her as he put on the thin one-piece garb; he knew that she was watching him, enjoying his shame. The white suit felt comfortable.

Forcing himself to turn around and look at her, he asked, "Why do you follow me?"

She looked out from under the rim of the hat, tilted her head back, and he noticed that the hat hid all her hair, if she had any; her eyes were very large. "From time to time," she said, "we're interested in seeing what you unchanged beasts have come to. Some others will look you over, then you'll stay with me." She smiled. "You can change too, if you want; of course you don't know what that means now, but you won't want to come back after you've seen the outside."

"What do you mean?" He was beginning to feel a vague fear.

She came up to him and closed the lock seam on the open chest of his new clothes. "You'll be like us," she said. He looked down at the smoothness of the fabric and wondered about the lack of buttons.

"Why should I want to be like an outsider?" he asked, looking up at her.

"Don't look so frightened—we were all here once, a long time ago. The whole world lived as you do, died as you do—"

"Outsiders took my mother."

"She's alive, somewhere. You won't have to die," she added.

He had heard that they would open his head, spill his blood, take away his pride, giving him pain and forgetfulness in return. He struggled with his fear, as it stole into his arms and legs, urging them to move: *hit her in the face and run.*

"If you run, I can catch you easily with my wheels. Old-fashioned, but fast."

He looked at his feet, and the fear he had never known made him tremble inside. "Please let me go on to the cave," he said without looking up. "If I am to die, let me die there, so that the one who comes after me may lead without fear. . . ."

She touched his arm. He looked up and saw the hairless skull of death smiling at him. She had taken off her hat, revealing her emaciation.

He tried to jump back, but she reached out and held him in place. He made a fist with his free right hand and swung at her face, but she pushed him away and he hit the sandy flat with his back. She fell on him before he could get up, spread-eagling him on the ground. Her eyes were soft and brown, examining him intently as she pressed herself down to hold him still. She blinked and smiled, eyes without eyebrows, skull bones set in pale flesh.

He shouted and tried to push up, but she hit him in the chest. Stunned, he lay still as she touched him through the seam of the suit. "Quiet now," she said, stroking him, "quiet." After a few moments she again closed the seam. "You're a wonderful beast. I'll want you for a long time."

He was gasping for air when she stood up and went back to her vehicle. She came back with a device of some kind strapped to her waist. She held another exactly like it in her right hand. Kneeling down, she lifted him into a sitting position and attached the small metal box to his waist, pulling at the device once to make certain it was joined to the suit. "We're going to fly," she said. She touched both boxes once and took his right hand in her left. Herdal felt himself lifted into the sky and hurled toward the high mountains. She turned her head to smile at him, and let go his hand. He cried out but did not fall. She drifted close to him and said, "You'll feel no cold or wind—we can go as high as we want."

The peaks were below them. His fear was gone as he stared down at the impossible ridges of rock and snow and valleys like plowed furrows. He tried to glimpse the trail that led to the cave of his ancestors, but it was too small and probably behind them.

There would be no bones for the one who came after him to arrange.

Sleep was a ship drifting on waves of darkness. Orbion could not open his eyes. A giant blue sun blazed in his dream-space, illuminating his insides with a cold, electric glare. The star burned upward into his brain, showing him the moisture-filled universe inside his body. The star pulsed with his heartbeat. Its life was his life. Slowly the personal sun brightened, turning yellower, whiter and hotter, permeating his body. The light coursed through his circulatory system, correcting time's deposit of random incoherence in cell structures. *I want to die, but only for a short while.* Light flowed through his nervous system, cleansing his brain—

He saw gangs of unchanged men breaking into the sleep centers to destroy the flasks. He saw himself waking at the end of time, crawling out of a damaged flask to silence and a blood red sun, knowing that they had forgotten to reanimate him. All of life was past now; he had missed it. A day in the springtime of creation was now worth more than a million years in a dying universe—

—and the sun was bloating into a giant red blot upon the sky; slowly the redness evaporated as seconds turned into ages, leaving only a small bright star which sent a chill through the cooling liquids of his body. Soon the star would give in to the closing hand of gravity, collapsing into a black cyst in space, locking up in a fist the energy it had once so freely given, until the moment when all space-time became one point readying to reveal a new unwinding of possibilities. . . .

"Do you wish to remember all your previous lives?" a voice asked.

"They hurt," he said.

"They can all be retrieved."

"It's enough that they are safely stored."

He trembled at the edge of an abyss, then fell and could not close his eyes.

Herdal became Rydpat, and lived three centuries. Rydpat became Kolem, who edited all his memories, forgetting Herdal. Kolem became Solion, who lived a thousand years without changing—his pride stopped him from admitting that he was bored with himself. Tooz, Esteb, and Versh lived a thousand years of borrowed lifetimes, inventing nothing, finally disappearing into the first Thrushcross. Anfisa, who had brought Herdal out of the wilderness, returned to the second Thrushcross as Evelyn, revealing that she was his mother from the time of Herdal, greeting him now through twenty lifetimes. Thrushcross revised himself for the third time after Evelyn told him that as Anfisa she had brought out his father, Rastaban. . . .

Stop, Thrushcross thought. *The past runs away like water.* A cool stream of water washed through his brain cells, removing small grains of unimportant memory, bits that would in time fill him to capacity with useless information. *"I don't want these memories,"* he said to the intruder. Life without end made one a sieve through which eternity flowed, each deposit of personal identity to be washed away by the next. The unchanged solved the problem through birth and death, through the peace of dissolution which followed too soon the pain of beginning. The unchanged accepted death as he welcomed passage in the sleep ship; the unchanged dead would never return again, but he craved the life to come, the returns to come.

He saw his body wrapped in yellow incandescence, the fine tracery of brain and nervous system visible as a whiter design. As the intensity of light increased, he felt himself dissolving into consciousness. His eyes ached to open. His ears strained to hear. His skin tingled warmly. Desire focused itself in his groin. His arms and legs sought to stretch. . . .

"Not yet, not yet," the intruder whispered in a hiss. *"Your life is not your own. The imagination of others, long gone, preys upon your life. You exploit urgently, ruthlessly, and are yourself exploited within a web of needs and contrasts spun from the irrational past still present in the lower structures of your brain—a*

brain still awash in an ocean of blood." Thrushcross saw a massive artery snaking down from a red sky into his chest. The voice was encamped in his center, as close as the protective illuminati. *"I will not be dislodged easily. That you will have to do for yourself, because I have bypassed your protectors."*

Silence. A memory quivered . . .

. . . *and the third Thrushcross became Tross* . . .

2-2 / Eyes of Satin, Rimmed with Gold

". . . this very abdication of human control over the direction of events might be regarded as a positive step by some, especially those who feel that the proper concern of mankind is the complex psychic world within each person. The desire to be master of one's fate is not universal . . . even in the West, where a few centuries ago this would have been regarded as dangerous heresy."

—GERALD FEINBERG, *The Prometheus Project*

All over the green countryside the stables were quiet, waiting for the dawn that would release their charges. Tross stood on the hillside watching the houses where the masters slept behind stone walls. He trembled slightly, startled by his own existence, his presence in the world at this very moment out of all possible moments, as if there had never been other moments, other places, other awarenesses turning inward in recognition; everything had just been created, including himself; the sense of the arbitrary, of the newness of things named only as he looked at them, was compelling. He was alive in a puzzle, trapped in a tide of things readying to follow this moment; he would act, and he felt the pleasure of anticipation, but he did not know what he was going to do next. The grass glowed in the morning night, drops of moisture still trembling with the light of steel-cold stars.

He lay down among the dew-laden blades and took a deep breath. Creepers groped toward his body, slowly attaching themselves to the fleshy valves on his arms and chest, filling his bloodstream with the liquid that held all knowledge of rooted, growing things. He felt his senses sharpen; he breathed in the fragrant festival of warming air wafting in ahead of the sun.

The grassy vines covered his body now, and he felt the movement of living things in the soil around him.

The sun pushed up slowly over the edge of the world, throwing a carpet of orange across the green land. The grassy vines withdrew as Tross breathed in the air of morning day. The dew dried from his body, leaving him washed and satisfied.

He stood up and went down to the villa below, through the open gate, across the court now flooding with light like a pool, through the open double doors into a room, surprising the waking lady as she lay naked in her bed. The master would by now be at the stable, preparing to release the beasts for the morning hunt of the unchanged, those who still lived in a chaotic freedom, resisting direction.

He fell on her just as she opened her three eyes, pushing up into her natural place. Her four arms beat on his back as he moved. She tried to squeeze his waist with her legs, stopping when she saw that it caused him no pain.

She was limp, resisting him with her contempt, glaring at him, trying to turn him to stone with her disdain.

He reached to her side and slipped his fingers into one of her orifices. It was moist and yielding between the ribs. With his left hand he found another on her left. Her face was without expression, but she almost cried out when yellow sunbeams cleared the court wall and shot into the room through the open double doors. He stopped and held her, as if she were wounded and her life was slipping away.

Her eyes were satin, rimmed with gold; the pupils were black. Her white hair flowed out of her head and fell back in a solid waterfall over the edge of the bed to the charge area terminal on the floor. His body tingled from the low level energy flowing through her body.

He thrust harder, using her side openings as handholds. She grew dewy in her sides; her face reddened and her lips parted to release a gentle puff of warm air. She closed her third eye, but left the two open, staring up at him. He heard a rush as she released a strongly scented musk. The fragrance quickened the flow of his blood to his muscles. He took deeper breaths as her arms began to stroke him lightly on his back and buttocks.

Suddenly her legs again encircled his waist. He felt the suction of openings near her navel, as they sought his valves. The short hairs of her soft white skin began to vibrate as she drew more power into her body, a million needles trying to pierce his skin.

Her breasts hardened. "Drink quickly," she said, "before I burst."

The sweet liquid pumped down his throat, sending fire into his limbs. As the flow stopped, his lips seized the other breast. In a few moments he felt swollen.

She grasped his head with two hands and guided his mouth to the openings under her breasts, forcing him to kiss the lips, first one and then the other. He drank the heat coming out of her, then tumbled into a cold abyss.

He shivered, grasping her back, grinding his palms into the bony hardness of her shoulder blades. She called to him in an endless procession of sounds, no two alike, leading him down a long corridor of musical notes.

A flood rose within him and filled her; but before he died she renewed his longing, suspending him again between desire and fulfillment. Eyes closed, he drifted in a blue space.

"He's back," she whispered, "but don't go!"

Tross opened his eyes, turned his head, and saw the figure standing in the doorway, just at the edge of vision. Pulling away from her, Tross turned on his back in time to see the tall leathery master rushing toward him, red lizard eyes open wide, blade raised to kill, as the lady began to laugh. . . .

3 / Flame of Life, Memory of Death

"Father, O father! what do we here
In this land of unbelief and fear?
The Land of Dreams is better far,
Above the light of the morning star."

—WILLIAM BLAKE

Thrushcross waded into the muddy water and pushed his way toward the island. He fell down once and his palms pressed down on the yielding bottom. He stood up and staggered forward, finally reaching dry ground.

He walked up toward the cylinder, through the open portal, and up a short ramp into a room lit in electric blue. Black cubes sat in a circle on the floor.

Thrushcross sat down on one of the shapes and the floor dissolved. He saw himself from above, standing near the tree, looking up at Evelyn's head. The interruption was over and the sequence was running forward again; the intruder had been eliminated.

Thrushcross felt himself flow into the nervous system of his simulacrum, while still watching the scene from above.

—the spear entered his chest, his attacker came at him with the machete, and his head flew upward—

Thrushcross withdrew as the simulacrum tumbled to the sand. He watched it bleed at the edge of the swamp.

He had looked through death more than once, tasting its supper of ashes, knowing that without it and its cousins, sleep and danger, there would be no quickening of sequences, no sharp edges, no welcoming of safety, no release of pleasure. The sight of his simulacrum faded from beneath his feet, ending the poem of death.

"Besides sensation there would be knowing," the intruder said, *"regions of music and reguli, without illusion."* Perhaps, after all, the intruder was part of the sequence?

"No. The sequence is not going forward. I have stopped it."

"You—who are you? Why do you intrude again? Where are you?" Thrushcross stood up from the cube and waited for an answer.

"Intrude? I have spoken and you have forgotten countless times, as you have forgotten identical lives, identical sleeps, endlessly alike returns."

"Where are you?"

"Right here." One of the cubes lit up inside, revealing a small frog-like body with four eye-stalks. The eyes were large globes filled with snow, regarding Thrushcross questioningly.

"Who are you?"

The light in the room brightened into warm crimson. "Later," the stranger said, "I'll tell you who I am." The voice was soft, louder than the previous thought-whispers. "Let me tell you a story. There will be a choice for you to make at the end, a choice you have never made before. After you have made it, I will tell you who I am. The choice will be one you will either forget or one which will make forgetfulness forever impossible, because you will leave the game cycles. I know this seems unclear to you, but it will be clear when I am finished." The four eye-stalks came together graciously.

Thrushcross sat down on the cube again and waited for the alien to speak. The forward eye-stalks floated slowly apart, one to each corner of the cube face, as if signaling some division of the subject at hand.

"When humankind reached a high level of control over biological materials five thousand years ago, intelligent life on Earth split into various branches . . ."

Suddenly Thrushcross thought that the transparent face of the cube was a prison wall, and the alien was speaking to him in desperation, each eye a human fist pounding from within.

". . . the relatively unmodified humanity left the Earth in mobile, self-reproducing worlds, societies which sought through new forms of social organization the attainment of individual happiness. The remaining unchanged clung to ancient ways, fearing any changes in the original organism; some of these still remain. Others accepted creative modifications, developing the gaming civilization. These are yours, seeking complex pleasures, successive lives, dramatic forms, the manipulation of the senses; all drawn from stored memory. You see, the position of individuals in ancient times was defined through a varying control of abundance and scarcity; after the great changes, when scarcity ceased to be a problem, the abundant life still reflected the natural life, vastly stylized, of course. Sequences varied in quality, from banal, anarchic creations given up to simple vitality, to fluid movements mirroring the will that moves all things. Yet even in the best could be seen the gesture of the beast, the pain of the fish swimming upstream to its spawning ground, the cruelty that does not know its own face . . ."

Thrushcross felt uncomfortable, nervous.

"You don't like standing aside from your game?"

"Why should I have to do it?" Thrushcross asked. "There's nothing of interest."

"Don't you feel curious? There are those who seek knowledge as the only way of life . . ."

"To examine like this," Thrushcross said, "to seek knowledge is for unchanged fools—the ancients showed us that it breeds a painful and unproductive self-consciousness, leading only to discontent. There is nothing beyond what I see and feel, and I will never know more."

"All you have is repetition, endless drifting . . ."

"I have not known it to be that."

"I will make you see it."

Thrushcross stood up, enjoying the anger which stiffened his body, curling his hands into fists. "I don't want you tampering with my sequence anymore. Who are you?"

"I study the forms intelligence has taken in the galaxy. The humankind left here on Earth, for example, is a strange mix of unconscious evolutionary residues and rational awareness; an exceptionally curious adaptation. Most races, when they reach the time of biological fluidity, choose a more cooperative, rational set of physical and social characteristics; these intelligences often leave the cradle of the home world to live in worlds of their own design, leaving the surfaces of natural planets to the unchanged, the inevitable portion of the naturally adapted for whom further change is a terrifying extravagance." The alien seemed to sigh for a moment; the eye-stalks quivered. "The debate follows a predictable form on countless worlds: in the name of humanism, or whatever name it goes by on a particular world, technical progress is denied; humanity saw basic flaws in itself once, faults which could not be remedied through technical progress or social reform. But if psychological forms become fluid, so do social and physical forms; there is no immutable nature and all the old objections are seen as brakes born of fear . . ."

"We please ourselves," Thrushcross said as he sat down again. "Now what is this choice of yours?"

"Look."

The floor dissolved again, revealing an endless deep of stars. Thrushcross leaned forward and fell on all fours, trying to press himself away from the openness of lanterned darkness. "That pale red star just below you," the alien said. "My world encloses that sun. I am a hybrid of intelligences from Earth and one other world. I offer you the choice of turning away from your life of endless returns and forgetfulness. I can give you clear, unbroken memory, with no accumulation of noise and useless impressions . . ."

Thrushcross managed to stand up and stagger back to the cube. "But why should I want to?" he asked as he sat down.

"If I were to open the gates of your suppressed memory, which still exists at basic levels in your brain despite removal techniques, you would see the endless sameness of your life, its poverty. Your society is trivial and changeless. Its existence is a problem to my understanding . . ."

"Why?"

"You do not direct your own lives."

"I don't care. Why should I listen to you?"

The eye-stalks seemed to look down, as if looking for the answer among the multitude of stars shining in space below the floor. "I cannot convince you by discussion alone," the alien said, "but I can affect you in ways that will help you understand . . ."

"I don't want to be affected," Thrushcross said.

". . . that you have no understanding of your past, hence no identity. Try to understand what I am saying. . . ."

Thrushcross considered for a moment. He saw a male face, a woman's face, children's faces, forest land, a small village.

"You were once an unchanged man," the alien said.

Thrushcross felt a silence inside him. In the stillness something entered his mind and began to direct his thoughts. He felt a new sense of power; a feeling of relief took hold of him. His protectors had come at last to help him. He began to answer the intruder.

"We have been freed from the chaos of reproduction, the pains of scarcity and competition, the limits of reality; we have created endless delight through simple physical health, friendships, and curiosity. Life for us is intentionally varied in ways we cannot predict; and we have destroyed death . . ."

"You must know that these are not your words," the alien said, "and that I am now speaking to the illuminati, not you."

"The illuminati lead, plan, and protect," Thrushcross said, "leaving us to our lives. All that was of the planning, shaping impulse in us lives in them. They are our other half. They are the living, incorruptible reguli of our lives, but they are part of us."

"But how do you know if what they do is right?"

"Their origins warrant our trust."

"You speak with more awareness, for the moment. But you will forget all this—"

"—as soon as I no longer need it."

"For you to see what I mean, Thrushcross, you would

have to divest yourself of the very controls and inputs that cannot be removed, since you have given up that choice. The illuminati feed you thought-toys, billowing dreams—"

"Do you have a name?" Thrushcross asked.

"Issli."

"You're very foolish, Issli, if you don't see that in your *mind* anything can happen; there can be no final difficulty, no restriction when all of material reality is made of thoughts."

"But in reality no species is omnipotent . . ."

"We don't have to be—except in ourselves. That is our great perfection. Your drab reality, with all its spaces and terrors, does not impinge—"

"—except through me, or through the natural catastrophes that one day will consume the Earth and sun."

"Why should I choose your life? What would I gain except restrictions?"

"You would gain a sense of reality and identity—the satisfactions of truth."

"Would there be happiness?"

"Only moments, but satisfaction and knowledge are more substantial."

"Your reality would not be very satisfying in its limitations, which is why the illuminati were created, and they built the frame of Earth for us to live in. Go away."

Issli was silent for a few moments. Thrushcross watched the eye-stalks come together over the body, as if trying to become one eye. "You assume," Issli said suddenly, "that your sequenced illusions are as real as the reality outside them—that you would perceive both in the same way, as well. Do you want to be wakened, to make the comparison, to see which world is the facade?"

"No. If you are right, it makes no difference. I don't

want to make the comparison. If I don't know, I won't know the difference. I now think my world vivid and interesting. Why should I spoil its intensity? We reject what you call reality, whatever it is. Whether you are telling the truth or a lie makes no difference."

"But the real world is profound, mysterious, inexhaustible."

Thrushcross felt nothing at the thought. "I want you to disappear," he said. "Even if you are right, we will in time reproduce all that your world contains. Now go away."

"But your powers do not reach that far . . ." The alien's body seemed to swell in a visible sigh. "It's always the same . . . the growing power over the physical environment leads to dimorphism . . . a species splits into those who leave the natural world, thereby extending knowledge, and those who stay to develop the unbounded energy of evolutionary flesh . . . the ones who leave choose the future of fate, of real limits painfully pushed back . . . the ones who remain choose the future of desire, which always finds a way of making failure feel like success. Desire is all will and inwardness, all that was cruel in screaming, competitive evolution, the central devil of all intelligent life in the universe. Those who leave natural planets, those seething caldrons of will boiling itself into first consciousness, first intelligence, meet other intelligences, thereby gaining an external viewpoint on their science and social organization; they gain a comparison of cosmologies, thereby satisfying in part their hunger for uncovering the nature of the universe. Their fate is the search for the given reality, which is multifarious. All these things you will never know."

"We create universes," Thrushcross said, "knowing that imagination is superior to all things outside it."

"Not true, not true," Issli said. "Fate will overtake your

world when the sun dies; or, if you should escape through the intervention of some kindly passerby, you will die when the cosmos dies."

"By then we will have placed all things inside ourselves." As he said the words, Thrushcross saw the stars and galaxies glowing inside his body; he would open his mouth and draw in all the suns shining at his feet, all the flowing darkness, all the worlds still awake . . .

"For you," Issli said, "there is nothing external; only the eye which sees a sight, a hand which feels. Your kind is quite insane. I am glad that you are not mobile."

Thrushcross felt distrust and fear. Words formed in his mouth: "There is no choice for me to make."

"Very well," the intruder said.

In a moment the cube was empty. The chamber darkened, leaving only the open doorway at the bottom of the ramp as a source of light.

3-1 / Resonance

"And what is good, Phaedrus,
And what is not good—
Need we ask anyone to tell us these things?"
—PLATO, *Phaedrus*

Outward, away from Earth's rivers and mountains, oceans and deserts, valleys and plains, across the Moon's orbital distance, the planet shrinking first into an oasis, then into a small green stone, finally becoming nothing, its locale marked by a fading star; across fleeing light-years to a world not grown in time's natural soil, a world which has captured its own sun within a shell: here Issli, ninth son of Earth, says, "I have returned." Even though he is used to space travel of one kind or another, he is not untouched by the vastness he has traversed.

Esteb, his co-researcher, asks, "What do you think?"

Issli's cube drifts out of the enclosure and settles to the floor. "They are a disappointing lot," he says.

Esteb brings his eye-stalks together and is quiet. Finally he asks, "Will we leave them to live as they do?"

Issli considers for a moment. "I think we'll have to . . . I don't know, maybe they know something we do not, though I was not able to find out what that might be. In any case, it will be wise to leave a reservoir of such worlds, to let them develop in their own way, just in case."

"But they do not develop—we've seen that again and again."

"I will consider them again one day."

"You seem affected."

"As one is affected by a story, a certain planned experience produced in the art forms of natural worlds. In these dramatic forms, experience was judged to be meaningful when it referred to some aspect of the real world, relating it to inner experience; but when reference was made only to the form, and imaginative fabrication—by which known sights and sounds of the culture were rearranged in some bizarre fashion—then the form became trivial and meaningless, a clever entertainment, lacking in all conviction. For us, the creation of beautiful things and the search for knowledge are the only things worth doing in the prison of the universe. Those of our brethren who still walk the Earth have chosen a terrible form of beauty—beauty without knowledge. They have no clear view of their condition in the cosmos. Are we who know better off? What shall become of us as we huddle around one star, then another? I don't know, but I am grateful for the openness of the question . . ."

And to convince himself he thinks: *in seeking happiness they forgot the virtues of satisfaction. Happiness is a bottomless pit, requiring infinite power with which to conjure. Thoughts become things, dreams reality—the cruelest wishes have no consequence, a river of stored information becomes flesh, solid material is projected to any part of the planet, data fed by the libido of endless power; and forgetfulness wipes away identity and all sense of good or evil. When the sun bloats into a red giant, this vast journeying of souls will scarcely notice the end of their billion-year playground. They will never have known the pursuit of knowledge, the satisfaction of curiosity, which requires great racial projects, the limiting of bodily energy through reason. They will never have known cumulative expansion, historically meaningful as a binding up of time, so that the latest may say, I am loyal to the first, and the last may feel kinship with all those who have gone forever into the dark . . . O Earth, I suffer with you in your blindness . . .*

"Let me tell you about our time-travel project," his companion starts to say and stops.

"There is no one to oversee," Issli says. "They have no one person or group which sees what they have come to. The interior life is all-pervasive and nothing else is known."

"Maybe we should wake them up," Esteb says.

"If we disturbed them, only the illuminati would speak to us, the ghosts they have set to rule. The humanity of Earth would be happy to dispense with physical objects completely; then they would not need the Earth. They would dream until all nature decayed. My friend, what prevents me from ignoring this form of life is the fact that too many intelligences in the galaxy engage in it for me to think it insignificant. Perhaps solipsism is a form of transcendent reference, like the ancient mathematics which relates the forms of all possible universes?"

"I think the dismissive posture is truest in this case," Esteb says.

"Theirs is a charming madness. Sampling it saddened me. Hoping to find something of myself in those who contributed to our form, I found only a crossroads . . ."

"There is not that much of their genetic input in our hybrid forms, Issli."

"If knowledge comes first, then perhaps I should have given myself up completely to their life before I could understand it."

"Not if it would mean a loss of consciousness. I would have to come and waken you—but you say that might not be possible."

"I would like to explore the memory of their artificial intelligences which circle the planet. Perhaps there is a record of some accident that brought a halt to all development, placing the entire society of immortals into a process of self-reference, a Moebius strip of self-awareness, producing the illusion of a high consciousness and new knowledge as the culture spiraled back into rearranged memories, internalizing all reality . . ."

"How could you even consider studying a circular system? There are enough other backward types which don't refute themselves so obviously."

"I thought there might be something I've overlooked," Issli says.

"Let me tell you about the new cosmology coming out of the equatorials . . ."

Issli floats out of his cube, and together with his companion drifts to the open view of their star, which is enclosed by millions of worlds, making up a porous shelf several astronomical units in radius. The worlds drink the yellow sun's energy and will continue to do so for as long as the sun's mass permits an outflow . . .

And Issli thinks: *Ultimately there is a universe out there which is not what we are; we may be made of the same stuff, but it is not what we are at our level of organization, the level of complexity that makes possible the qualities of intelligence and self-awareness. We fail to grasp this universe at its most basic levels of organization; when we try, we alter, splintering reality. Yet we know something of it, even if we cannot be its complete masters. This surely must be better than denying the difference between a self-reference inwardness and the vast sea around us which crystallized our forms . . .*

"There is something of Earth in you," Esteb says, "in the way it draws you, in the way you are troubled."

As he looks across the sun's intimate space, at the many-shaped worlds set in a globular mesh around it, Issli worries about the resonances created in his mind by the visit to Earth. *A zoo of strange lives. Many a culture leaves such living relics behind it in the climb away from the mad vitality of origins. Earth is a place of rituals, illusory knowledge and false wisdom . . .*

And something in me loves its desperate beauty.

4 / Memory Is No More

"If a man could be sure
That his life would endure
For the space of a thousand long years—"

—SONG

"Add and alter many times,
Till all be ripe and rotten;"

—ANONYMOUS

"But even at 'death's end' men will remain finite

beings in their accomplishments if not their expectations. I do not know whether the opportunity to exercise our abilities over an indefinite time period will itself be an answer to the unhappiness over our finitude. . . . If this should not prove the case, then some other kind of reconstruction of man appears called for to deal with finitude."

—GERALD FEINBERG, *The Prometheus Project*

Shapes stood in the sky, morning clouds outlining a pair of vast, contemptuous intelligences scrutinizing the landscape. Thrushcross sat on the terrace looking out over the plateau, waiting for the end, for the sleep that would renew him. Sometimes he sat here at night, when the world was lit by lightning, each flash a spider of electricity as it moved away from him over the Earth. Mornings he would lean over the small table, setting down marks on the rolls of white parchment, noticing the leatheriness of his hands and the white hairs from his head touching the table. His eyes hurt at the end of each day, and he wondered why renewal was taking so long. When he slept, his dreams were filled with sharp stones, and he felt that he had failed to complete some task. Daily he set down the red marks, imagining that they represented a vast cycle of musical sounds, and he would hear them played during his next return to life.

The red notes flowed endlessly from his hand, more varied and complex as he cut the roll into sheets. The protectors had failed to take him into the sleep ship. The illuminati had forgotten that he had lived past his measured sequence. Throughout the world, he knew, others were passing into new lives, leaving him to die like one of the unchanged.

He looked out over the grassy plateau below his Earthen

terrace set in the mountainside, and beyond to the lowlands. Suddenly his eyes filled with tears, and he longed to enter the landscape, transfigure every particle of it with his own consciousness; every tree, stone, blade of grass and grain of sand would become an aspect of himself.

Gone would be the terrible isolation of waiting, of looking down at the red marks whose meaning lay just beyond his grasp. . . .

Moments passed. A cool breeze touched his face, drying his tears. A sudden realization of his own existence surprised him. He looked down again at the characters on the parchment. They seemed to writhe as he tried to read their meaning, transparent snakes filled with blood, an endless, animated frieze of memory, each echo unrecognizable, empty, except for the pain he felt.

Clouds passed, uncovering the sun's warmth. His sense of self was slipping away. He closed his eyes and watched shapes glide across a bloody background. When he opened them, he did not know what he was seeing. Light flooded his field of vision. He looked at his hand and found it strange, as if he had picked up an oddly shaped piece of wood at the shore. He had no name, no shape, only a waking awareness. He was concealed in time, in a grain of sand in a river bed, as the water rolled on. He looked out through eyes as hard as glass, feeling an empty attentiveness that craved to be filled.

I want to be a child again, naked, without knowledge or memory. He remembered a choice, a chance at renaming the universe, and he had chosen memory, endless desire, possible only in the world at the center of his will. The illuminati knew his will. They would provide and protect. *I want to die, but only for a short time.* A bell knelled somewhere like a broken wail.

He leaned forward and saw his father coming up the path to the house. Evelyn walked with him, brushing away the foliage that threatened to cover the clay path. At last they were coming to take him to the sleep ship; at last Thrushcross began to feel again the tug of time, drawing him forward into a new private place, among endless places to come. Rastaban and Evelyn were youthful and smiling as they walked in the lush greenery.

Thrushcross closed his eyes. A prayer of understanding entered his mind. *Death once gave renewal. We die by degrees, discarding memories, keeping what we please of ourselves. We renew our bodies without the sacrifice of death. We shape ourselves. We go on despite forgetfulness.* The pen dropped from his hand and he leaned back in his chair. His will expanded to fill the world, until such time when it would again fall back into the limits of individual awareness. Memory rushed away from him, emptying into an infinite sea, where all things were possible, where all distinctions were obliterated, all pain dissolved. . . .

Emtio awoke. He turned his head and saw two faces watching him from behind the clear partition, a man and a woman. *I remember, I remember,* he thought as the faces turned away and disappeared from sight.

Between the Winds

Inside (1)

The sun was a bloody Portuguese man-of-war sinking into the tar-black sea. Ishbok leaned on the ship's wooden rail and was suddenly afraid that the world would disappear if he stopped thinking about it.

The sea sloshed against the horizon as if it were the rim of a bowl. He tried to remember leaving port. Perhaps his memory had been affected by his best friend's death at the hands of the mad street prophet. What was his friend's name? The same as the poor soul who had been washed overboard by the storm yesterday. Or had it been the day before?

Ishbok squinted as the wind struck his face with a million pinpricks, and was grateful for the sudden reality of the sensation. The rain, still some leagues off, dropped a gauzy curtain on the sunset, obscuring something dark moving on the horizon, pushing through an invisible barrier at the edge of the world, as if coming in from the sky.

A serration of waves cut across the crimson blister of the setting sun.

The whale-thing swam closer. Ishbok gripped the rail as he saw black armor plate. Time twitched forward.

His vessel's lower deck guns fired; white smoke billowed into the dusk from the lower deck as thunder pulsed in his belly. The iron whale swelled until he could see its great round windows, eyes furious with fire, and he staggered back as it struck the ship. Ripping vibrations shot up through his feet. He swung around, coughing from the smoke, and the deck tilted, pitching him over the rail. He struck the whale-thing, rolled on the metal plates clawing for a handhold, then slipped off and tasted the sea. Surfacing, he saw the whale-thing tear through his ship.

He cried out to his crew as the current bore him away, and realized they had been trapped below on the gun decks as the ship went down.

Light drained from the world as the last red sliver of daystar was eclipsed by the horizon, and the sea seemed to boil as if quenching the sun. The sky filled with musing stars. Rock raked his back. He turned around and saw a tower of stone reaching up into the night. Probing with his arms in the water, he crawled forward on the submerged crags, hands and knees slipping on the seaweed as he struggled to stand up into the cool air.

At last he scrambled out of the water, sat down on the rough rocks and watched the woolly clouds glide in from the north. Stars pierced the overcast for a while, their glitter fading and dying as they were drawn into the net of obscurity.

I am alive, he said within himself, shivering in the salt spray, searching the gloom, feeling desolate and lost. The world wore a mask, and imposed forgetfulness on his thoughts and suspicions as they arose. He shuddered, slipping toward numbness as chill breezes rushed through him. He looked up and saw a star struggling to penetrate the clouds, burning bright as if hoping to ignite the cottony cumulus.

I am alive, he repeated within his cavernous self, *but the universe has walls.*

Lightning joined sea and sky, thunder tore the air. He

rose and saw the echo of the timeship cutting through the clouds, then fading.

Time tumbled backward, and he almost remembered.

Outside (1)

Eighteen thousand years after the mobiles had left Earth, the first to return found a deserted planet, growing back green, except for one large structure plunging deep into the plain of what had once been central North America. They worked all day to open the random molecular locks to enter the inner chamber of worlds inside the pyramid.

The chamber, a brightly lit sphere at the center of the double pyramid, housed thousands of shining blue globes, stored rigidly against each other in large, skeletal container frames set on a polished floor that cut the chamber in half.

Gibby, a youth not yet a century old, who had studied with deep fascination the report of the technical team that had been here a week earlier, caressed one of the balls with the palm of his hand. "Every one of them," he said, "is a world of living, feeling people who have existed in virtual dreams for so long that they accept them as the real world. They're just as much lost as the people of generation starships we've encountered, who no longer know that they exist on a ship or that it has a destination."

"And what shall we do, Gibby?" asked Gorrance, the linguist. "Disillusion them?"

"We can't do that," Gibby replied, irritated by the fact that she had already made up her mind. Her millennium of life, he told himself, had not made her infallible, although she sometimes seemed to believe it had.

"Why not?" Gorrance asked, her dark eyes narrowing.

"Why not disillusion them? Mentalities that fail to distinguish between fantasy and reality need our help—if we can even say that we're dealing with real persons of any kind—to be put out of their misery."

"There's no point in disillusioning them," said Kateb, the head of the expedition. He was nearly half Gorrance's age, but she still treated him as a child. "We've come here only to observe a noumenal humanity that once had something in common with us."

"Yes," Gorrance said, "before they moved into their dreams!"

"There's a control center here," Gibby said, moving eagerly to a series of round touch-panels, above which stood three large square tanks, each black inside as if filled with a viscous liquid. "Shouldn't there be bodies stored somewhere?"

"There was nothing in the technical survey," Gorrance said. "It seems they moved inside permanently, abandoning their bodies."

Gibby was studying the panels, pressing control surfaces and anxiously waiting to see if any of the tank monitors lit up, realizing that there would be stored physical bodies only if anyone wanted to come out. These people might have left a way out only at first, and had then decided to go inside permanently.

As the three tanks began flickering, Gibby looked around the chamber, feeling almost as if a virtual caretaker might appear. A foolish notion: these systems had certainly been designed to maintain themselves.

Kateb frowned. "The trouble with sub-creations," he said, "is that they can't escape the cosmology of the external world in which they are embedded. A sun may go nova and collapse into a black hole, a planet might be destroyed by collisions—virtuals are vulnerable and can't do anything to save themselves."

Gorrance said, "Yet countless fools have claimed that virtual worlds might be the equal of given reality, and maybe preferable to it. I've seen this kind of thing before. Once it was a planetary colony, where life got too hard. Another time it was an interstellar vessel, adrift because of some malfunction, with no one left alive except in the virtual banks. It could happen to any culture."

Gibby did not want to hear again about the difference between virtual worlds and the reality that impinged on senses and instruments from outside. He had heard enough about genuine, uncreated otherness. It did not mean that virtual insides were necessarily simple creations. That depended on the sophistication of the creators.

"I wonder," he said, gazing into the blank noisy holo monitors before him. "Is there really an outside? Have we ever been able to look that far? Maybe the settings of our senses, on which even our best instruments depend, are no different in principle from the settings of virtuals. Perhaps we don't move through space at all, as we imagine that we did in coming here, but through a vastly rich mental space. We're all inside."

He liked the idea, whether it was true or not.

"Nonsense!" Gorrance cried. "Which of us would dive into a sun? We are not dreams! Even the insiders must have believed in their own given reality before they entered their hells."

"But they also had to believe in the hard won reality of their creations," Gibby objected, "before committing themselves irrevocably."

All three holo-tank monitors lit up suddenly in front of Gibby, casting a blue glow across the chamber. "Now we'll see how they live," he said excitedly as Gorrance and Kateb came up, and together they watched the images that began to move inside the center tank. . . .

Inside (2)

Ishbok raised his head from the field of battle. Black horsemen searched through the sunset glare, silencing the cries of the wounded with quick lance-thrusts. Thirsty, burning with pain, he lay back on the parched plain and remembered the ages still to come, when an ice shrouded Earth, cold and clean, would emerge into a flowering green spring. . . .

"We can't take anything with us," he had said in futurity to the love of his life.

Reproach hid in Aina's eyes.

"There's no room," he insisted. "The ship will only take people."

She tried to look cheerful. "Do you think we'll ever come back here?"

"To a later time, perhaps, when our scouts find the end of the ice. Not much may be left here by then. It's best to go to empty places in the past, so we won't inconvenience anyone."

. . . and a lance struck through a body near him. He looked up at the first evening stars, and the icy Earth trembled in his memory as he waited to be pierced. Black lightning rushed across the whiteness toward the timeship. Deep crevasses opened in the glacier as people struggled to board the black, sluglike vessel to escape the coming ice age. The ship rippled in his eyes, as if already slipping through time, cutting off the line of people trying to board. Then it solidified and stood brutishly on the ice, as if fixed for all eternity, having no need to timeslip.

The sky began to glow.

"Aina!" he cried out. Her eyes were wild as she struggled to reach him through the crowd. The moment became infinitely long, refusing to end, and he held onto it desperately as he waited for his time here to expire.

Outside (2)

"Such intense feeling," Gibby said with awe as he peered into the center tank. "He's dying in one place and reliving his life in another."

"Life?" Gorrance asked contemptuously, but with a touch of pity. "These effigies and simulacrums aren't truly alive."

"Inside, you would feel alive," he answered, "as much as you feel being here and mocking these beings. These spheres are human colonies, living as they have chosen. It has to be so. There could have been no doubt that it was a desired way of life before so many went inside."

"We don't know that," she said, "and I don't see how we ever could. As far as we know they're just recordings, developing along random probabilities in a system that has gone chaotic, from what we see. If they were alive, I'd be for erasing them, to put them out of their pain. They're living in a mill that cannot ever be as rich as the natural universe, which we have never exhausted. Face it, Gibby, this is what's left of a cultural disaster."

Gibby knew the historical scenario well enough, but felt uncertain about the conclusions and judgments drawn from it. Thousands of years ago, when faced with so-called virtual creation, nanotechnology, and the laying of information highways, branches and offshoots of humankind had succumbed to creative subjectivity. Rather than affecting the reality around them by rebuilding their solar system, or reaching out to the stars in self-reproducing mobiles, these planet-bound folk had moved into their dreams in a fatal way—by linking the output of their minds, through dream generators, to their input, which gave them the experience of omnipotence—believing they could have all they could imagine, all that they had ever lost, for as long as the instrumentalities continued to function and the river of energy did not run dry.

"All cultures are dreams," Gibby said, examining the controls more closely, "cysts embedded in a frame of nature, which sets our initial biases through evolution. Why should we not throw nature off and make our own way? Our own mobile culture is also a dream within an indifferent universe. What you call reality is merely one kind of dream."

"Come, come, Gibby," Kateb said. "You sound as if you'd like to live in these nodules. Can't you see that it's all gone wrong? It's incoherent."

"Maybe it's what they wanted," Gibby said, turning away from his teammates to gaze into the second holo tank, where clouds and human figures were drifting into view . . .

Inside (3)

Ishbok tumbled, drifting above the towers. The wind howled in his ears as the horizon drew him and the blue sky invaded his eyes and opened the infinity at the back of his mind.

Countryside appeared below. He slowed, stopping the sun, feeling its light go cold on his face as he recovered his sorrow.

Then he searched the sky for other survivors. A few motes drifted above him, but he could not see their faces. He tried to pull them toward him, but they resisted, and finally clouds obscured his view.

He recalled the days of departure, a month after the solar system's entrance into the deadly cloud of interstellar debris. Meteor trails had crossed the sky like glowing raindrops on a window, becoming larger with each incoming wave, until they broke the glass.

"It's hopeless," he had told Aina. "There are countless larger fragments in the cloud, rushing head-on toward us. At best we'll have a long winter. At worst, the Earth will be shattered by a large fragment. Nothing to come back to, ever."

"Are there big fragments?" she had asked achingly.

"Yes," he had answered.

"But we can jump a billion years!" she had exclaimed, and suddenly he could not remember what else she had said or what had happened to her. Time stopped, trapping him between memories.

Outside (3)

"You're blind, Gibby!" Gorrance said, gesturing with both hands as if fending off a physical attack. "How can you be fooled by all this?"

Startled by her uncharacteristic vehemence, Gibby frowned and said, "You can have what you want inside. From what we might learn here, we might be able to perfect a new form of existence."

"We can't rewrite physical laws, or abolish the structure of an infinite universe."

"Why not? Perhaps if we reach deeply enough, we'll find the innermost chaos, the ground from which even the outermost may be reshaped."

"Delusions!" Gorrance shouted. "You've forgotten how all this must have happened, when this culture, like others, simply forgot the difference between amusement and reality. Entertainment gave them their deepest, darkest wishes, without any obvious cost. Violence, brutality, the heartless torment of other human beings, the wringing of every pleasure from power and sexual adventure—all supplied free of conscience and remorse."

Gibby felt pride at having provoked her. The issue had to be important for her to react with such intensity. Perhaps she thought something of him after all.

Gorrance calmed down and looked at him with concern. "Their escapes were crude at first," she continued. "They had only their games, books, paintings, their dramas, all of which could verge on becoming life itself, or the most important thing in it. No culture can live in both realms for long, without one subverting the other. Too much reality, and creativity dies. Too much imagination, and reality dies."

Gibby was silent, knowing that Gorrance would not let him answer until she was finished.

"The struggle went on, life contending with reinvented life. Every civilization that survives the early threats of tribal warfare will have to contend with the temptation of dreams—and here the lure of wishes has won out, as it did elsewhere. I expect to see it too often, this exile of intelligent life to an inward shore, spreading across hermetic empires, where new generations will accept artificialities as reality—caves on whose walls will creep the shadows of blind and lost humanities, tyrannized by artificial intelligences." She gazed past him at the tanks. "We can't even call them generations, really. They are the deathless copies of once living personalities proliferating through the matrix."

Gibby gave her a disappointed look.

"Of course all cultures have had ways of hiding out from the universe," she continued. "Communal caves in which we give ourselves faces and names without knowing who we are, and give up asking the hard questions."

"You like the questions," Gibby said, "more than the answers. You won't accept any answer that isn't part of the question. Who are we?"

Gorrance narrowed her eyes. "You know that we strive to be acultural, pursuing only knowledge, trying to understand who we are—if that question has any meaning. We are what we make of ourselves, after we have understood how nature made us."

"Have we ever succeeded to any degree?" Gibby asked.

Gorrance frowned. "As well as I can see, we have to be a question mark, floating free of evolutionary niches and conventional cultures, avoiding the rigidity that the ancients too often saw as identity. We are nothing, but remain free to develop and grow, to abandon and begin again, looking outward as much as inward. We don't ask who we are, because a sense of identity cannot be bestowed. We know our origins, and we continue to grow and change—a work in progress."

"I've heard all this," Gibby said.

"And you question it."

"I sometimes long to be something much more specific."

"You long to enter one of these locked worlds," she said with cold disappointment.

"Yes," Gibby said eagerly, gazing at the controls. "So I can have exactly what I want." He felt himself tremble, as if a great chord had suddenly been struck deep within him. "I want to see what it feels like, at least for a while."

Gorrance shook her head. "You won't have that, ever, because these worlds, however vivid, must have a horizon, a mechanical rigidity. They can't equal the unpredictability of an open, standing infinity in which local universes are random fluctuations, single possibilities in an infinity of possibilities. You would be choosing only a sub-creation of a sub-creation, a cave within a cave. At worst, you would simply die and never know it, and a caricature of you would appear in the tank. At best, you would emerge into a universe that is much more limited than our own. And you would certainly not be able to come out."

Gibby shook his head in denial and gazed around the chamber of worlds. "I'll see for myself."

Gorrance looked at him with concern and said, "There will be nothing of you left to bring out, and it may not be you who will see, but a poor simulacrum."

Inside (4)

The agony of his loss flared through Ishbok, and he recalled that some had left the planet, fleeing uselessly to other communities within sunspace. Others, unable to abandon their beloved Earth, had slipped into the past, swimming against the currents of entropy's river to earlier, brighter times. Down from the infinitely branching future to beginnings, the ship was a ghost passing through all possible worlds, seeking sunny moments in the vast uninhabited stretches of time's estates. . . .

He held Aina's hand. The lake was a silver mirror spilling streams into a green forest. The timeship hovered in a tall sky, preparing to land, then was caught between the winds of branching possibilities and torn apart, scattering its people into the vortex, leaving them to echo with aspiring reality in the varying timestream. Yearning for fixity, flickering dust motes fought dissolution with fragments of memory, struggling to halt drift and self-cancellation. The inertia of unknowing opposed waves of suffering remembrance, reminding him that the survivors, robbed of continuity, would drill and fade forever, echo begetting echo, fainter into infinity, spiraling in toward the unattainable singularity of nonbeing. . . .

Outside (4)

"You just don't understand," Gibby said. "I want to experience omnipotence, even if it's illusory."

Kateb shook his head. "To hear this from one of us means there must be deep flaws in us." He was looking sternly at Gibby. "Even twenty thousand years of self-design and redesign haven't eliminated them, it seems."

"You misunderstand," Gorrance said. "Gibby's perversity only proves our continuing openness, even if he chooses to end it for himself."

"What would I be ending?" Gibby asked, intrigued by Gorrance's half-hearted defense of him. "This reality you bow before is imposed on me. I never chose it."

"But it is infinitely more creative than what you'll find inside."

"Perhaps—but it can't give me the experience of omnipotence, to change my world at will."

"If this system is still functioning correctly," Kateb added. "You may not get what you want. And remember, your body will be a problem after your mental algorithm is recorded and engaged. There may be no coming back—except if you imagine it."

"Which you won't be able to do," Gorrance said, "because the whole point is to forget the artifice, to believe in the reality, to be fooled completely, to be a complete fool."

"But I won't know that," Gibby said, "and I will have what I want. The experience is all that counts. I can only doubt and suffer *before* I go inside."

"And if you don't find what you want?"

"I may feel that I have even if I don't. I'll traverse this hall of worlds for what may be a subjectively infinite time."

"Until this sun dies," Kateb said, "revealing the lie of subjective worlds."

"I won't know it when that happens."

"But you know it now," Gorrance said. "Keep in mind that during the transfer only your copy may go inside, leaving you outside and possibly injured. Gibby, you don't really want to take the chance, do you?"

"I didn't think about that," Gibby said.

Kateb said, "Perhaps we should destroy this place, so others won't be tempted."

"No!" Gibby cried.

"These worlds are a waiting addiction," Gorrance added.

Kateb raised a hand. "We'll catalog them first, maybe see if we can communicate with them—"

"These are not living cultures from which we can learn

anything. They're only elaborate kaleidoscopic hells in which the echoes of the living suffer, not worlds in which to open embassies."

"But can we destroy them?" Gibby asked. "Complete erasure may be impossible."

"We'll destroy the whole physical matrix," Gorrance said. "This is only the lingering ghost of a culture. No one is left on the planet. The originals perished long ago."

"Why not just leave what's left alone?" Kateb asked.

"That may be more cruel than destruction. These insides are obviously drifting into chaos. You can see how bits and pieces of persons are trying to use what control they have to make sense of their world."

"But surely the builders knew the dangers," Gibby protested, "and the provisions for correction."

"No safety device can last forever," Kateb said.

"Is it possible that everything may be working just fine," Gibby asked, "even though it looks wrong to us?"

Kateb looked at Gorrance. "He still wants to go inside."

"It's his decision," she said resignedly. "I can't believe he wants it, but it must be his free choice. We can't force him to do what's best, even if he fails, much as I'm tempted to save him."

"I wonder," Gibby said, "why these monitors are here. Was someone meant to watch?"

Kateb said, "The monitors were probably guides for new arrivals."

"I'll watch for a while," Gibby said, "before I decide."

As Gorrance and Kateb turned to leave, he turned his gaze to the row of open, coffin-like receiving chambers that stood to the left of the tanks.

"I pity you," he heard Gorrance say behind him, surprising him with the sorrow in her voice.

Inside (5)

Ishbok was slipping from the rock into the sea, drawn by powerful, conflicting currents that stopped and started in discrete steps.

Why was I not given something else to be? he asked, clinging to the rock that seemed to rise and fall with the waves. He felt that he was dying and being reborn from second to second. Finally, he felt continuous, and stood up in the wind.

The echo of the timeship appeared low over the water and passed through him, ripping the sight of cloudy sky from his eyes and streaking the stars. Aina's giant shape rose from the sea, picked him up from the rock, and hurled him skyward.

He floated, weak, unbreathing, clawing at the vacuum, unable to die. Space crumpled up like paper around him; his awareness collapsed to a point in the darkness, but he resisted nothingness.

I am alive, he whispered, echoing within himself, *alive, alive, alive* as his world crushed him into an endless limbo—and he found himself walking across a large grassy clearing, in the center of which sat the timeship. People were coming down the gangway in small groups. He stopped and watched them, feeling the bright sunlight on his face. Aina came out and saw him at once. She waved. He waved back and hurried toward the ship, feeling that he had been in peril somewhere else only a few moments ago. . . .

Outside (5)

Gibby came out of the great pyramid and started across the field, to where the exploratory flyer waited three hundred meters short of the forest. The day was sunny, so vividly real that he was taken aback by its immediacy, and he almost dropped the small globe he carried. The landscape was as much inside him as outside, possessing both depth and opacity beyond his senses, where he knew it was entirely different from what he perceived, an ethereal wave function supporting the varied experience of space-time. One might break out of a virtual space and ruin its reality, but how would one break out of the space around virtual space into the noumenal space that supported the realm of phenomena? It could not be done, however one tried to imagine the noumenal.

Gorrance and Kateb were right, of course. The infinite, uncreated universe around him was a transcendent fact that could not be contained in any finite mind; and rather than taking it as an affront to his pride, he should accept it as a happy, miraculous gift.

There was nothing here on Earth for him and his kind, he realized as he came up to the flyer. Gorrance and Kateb were waiting for him, sitting cross-legged in the tall grass.

"What took you?" Gorrance asked, standing up and smiling, unable to hide the fact that she was glad to see him. Then she saw the globe in his hand and her eyes narrowed.

"It wasn't going right for them inside," he said. "I made some changes, so the survivors might be reunited in a better time. And I took two of them out with me, a man and a woman. I'll re-embody them when we get home, as a test of what Gorrance said about their limits."

She gazed at him sadly. "Even when you talk to them in the flesh, they'll be only mechanical analogs of persons, not alive at all. And you'll have to destroy them—"

Gibby felt a surge of objection. "Ah, but what if they are people, and pass all the hurdles of subtlety? What will you say then, Gorrance?"

"No, no!" she said. "You'll see right through them. Their world's initial conditions were intrinsically impoverished, incapable of generating depth and complexity."

"We'll see," Gibby said. "Maybe something new was achieved here. Maybe we can improve on it and learn to create. Maybe we can build a secondary universe that will be independent . . ."

"Impossible," Gorrance said with a wave of her hand. "No secondary world can equal the primary's complexity, because the primary exists in a transcendent infinity which can only be simulated, never duplicated. A perfect illusory world would be a real world—and there can only be one—" She looked into Gibby's eyes. He felt her strength flow into him, and realized that she cared about what he thought, how he thought, and would continue to pity him if he failed to reason clearly. Her words had stopped him from going inside, but something deep within him continued to resist her, as if she had stolen something from him.

Kateb stood up and said, "We'd better go," then gazed up at the giant pyramid and sighed. "It's only an antique way, full of style and feeling, slowly losing whatever grace it had. We came from here, but there's nothing left but ghosts in a tomb."

"What if you're wrong, even in part . . ." Gibby started to say, gazing at the ball in his hand, aware that he was still denying the tragedy of the situation, "then you've tried to discourage me from playing a merciful god."

"And *that's* what you wanted?" Gorrance asked softly.

"Yes," he said, closing his hand around the ball.

"Transfigured Night," copyright © 1978 Jack Dann. From *Immortal*, edited by Jack Dann. Harper & Row, Publishers, Inc., N.Y. 1978.

"Wayside World," copyright © 1977, 1985 George Zebrowski. Reprinted, with revisions, from *A World Named Cleopatra*, produced by Roger Elwood, Pyramid Books, N.Y. 1977.

The employees of Five Star hope you have enjoyed this book. All our books are made to last. Other Five Star books are available at your library, through selected bookstores, or directly from us.

For information about titles, please call:

(800) 223-1244

or visit our Web site at:

www.gale.com/fivestar

To share your comments, please write:

Publisher
Five Star
295 Kennedy Memorial Drive
Waterville, ME 04901